TO CATCH A FALLEN STAR

June B. Anderson

Copyright © 2008 by June B. Anderson

To Catch A Fallen Star
by June B. Anderson

Printed in the United States of America

ISBN 978-1-60477-803-8

All rights reserved solely by the author. The author guarantees all contents are original and do not infringe upon the legal rights of any other person or work. No part of this book may be reproduced in any form without the permission of the author. The views expressed in this book are not necessarily those of the publisher.

Unless otherwise indicated, Bible quotations are taken from The New King James Version. Copyright © 1979, 1980, 1982 by Thomas Nelson, Inc. Used by permission.

www.xulonpress.com

ACKNOWLEDGMENTS AND DEDICATION

To God the Father, and my Savior, Jesus Christ–You trusted me to write this, and I'm trusting You to build Your kingdom with it. I promised You from the beginning that this and everything else I will ever write will be for You to do with as You see fit. I haven't changed my mind. Take it...it's Yours. First and foremost it is dedicated to You.

When I felt like God was prompting me to write this book, it was just our little secret, God's and mine. For whatever reason. When I decided to let my family in on it, they were so encouraging and asked me how it was going from time to time. When the first draft was completed, I asked my husband, son, and daughter to read it and honestly critique it. Their opinions were of enormous importance to me, so I gave them each a copy and the freedom to "mark it up" however they felt led. I only asked them to be nice about it! I really feel like they gave me their honest opinions, and for that I am truly grateful. Thank you, my dears, so very much. To my son and daughter: Those AP English classes finally paid off, huh? To my husband: It wasn't the grind I thought it would be to you!

My darling husband, you are a rock and definitely my brains when my own seem to fail me. Your intelligence amazes me (and everyone else) and your constant desire to help me with any project I have is unbelievable. You are such an encouragement to me, not only in writing but also in life. If I had not had your approval on this labor of love, I'm not sure how God would have gotten me through it, I only know He would have; but you gave not only your approval but your ALL in seeing this come into being. You made it so much easier for Him and me...not that His arm is *ever* too short. I love you more than you will ever know.

My darling daughter, you are a rock and my example of a fighter. Over the years you have taught me to never give up and never let anything get the best of me. You are infinitely stronger than I have ever been. When you were that precious little pixie in pink I thought you would forever be my little delicate petunia, but you have become a vigorous rose standing tall, strong, and beautiful, and even though roses have thorns, it is a rarity indeed if anyone pricks a finger on yours. Protect those thorns, though. You'll need them. You are the voice on the stage, singing and proclaiming God's Word, that I only dreamed of and could never be. That is an irreplaceable treasure to me. I would say that I love you more than you will ever know, but since you will soon be birthing my first grandchild, I have a feeling it won't be long before you know EXACTLY how much I love you.

My darling son, you are a rock and a constant reminder to me of my need for stability and encouragement, for you are a stabilizer and a kind exhorter. You never let me forget that if people dream, they should dream big. All along the way in bringing this project to fruition, when I faltered, you believed. When I doubted, you believed. You are the hands on the instrument, keeping time to God's music, that I never could have been. That, too, is an irreplaceable treasure to me. When you were little, I had no idea that my painfully shy little towhead would become the bold handsome young man that you are. I can see you becoming the husband God is calling you to be to that wife I keep telling you that God is preparing for you. I love you more than you will ever know until, like your sister, you have a child of your own.

My darling son-in-law, you are a rock and an example of faithfulness. You love my daughter with an everlasting love, and I am so grateful to God that she has you. I know if I had asked you to read and critique the first draft, you would have, but I also know that your job requires much of you, including lots of reading, and I just couldn't ask you to do more. Just knowing that you are supportive (and allowed your wife to escape to her place of refuge so she could read it) means more to me than you can know. I love you more than you will ever know until the little one arrives; then, as I said to your wife, you will know.

A wall can not be built with just one rock, but with many rocks a strong fortress can be built. Knowing that I am the wimp among them all, Jesus has allowed in my life these family members who are strong, each in his or her own way. They are a wall of protection for me...a strength...and each has as his or her own foundation THE Rock, Jesus Christ, the Son of God. For that, I don't have enough words of gratitude to God, so I simply bow my heart before Him and say, "Thank You, Lord."

To my beautiful friend Phyllis, I can't thank you enough for accepting the challenge to read the second draft and critique it. I feel like you were honest, and you just can't know how much I appreciate that. You, my dear, are also a rock, having defeated, in the Name of Jesus, breast cancer and other mountains in your life. You have demonstrated for all to see, more than once, what it takes to be a true Christian, full of grace. All people who face adversity should follow your shining example. I love you more than you know.

For all the reasons stated above, this book of hope is dedicated to my little family and my friend Phyllis. God bless you all, now and forever.

CHAPTER ONE

All the way to the airport Holly Monroe clutched her small red purse and made jokes about whatever came to mind...her outfit, her hair style, the notion that the weather would probably be horrible in The Netherlands, and other items of useless chatter.

The Netherlands...why had she chosen The Netherlands? Oh, yes, the tulips and the cheese. Tulips were her favorite flower, and she had always wanted to visit The Netherlands when they were in bloom. She wanted to see fields full of them. Acres and acres. All colors...one color...it didn't matter. And cheese? Well, The Netherlands is famous for cheese, too, and besides...it's food. And she did love to eat. Thankfully, she had a pretty decent metabolism, so whenever she put on a couple of pounds, they were easily removed. Fortunately, they only collected around her middle, therefore they were easy to hide. *I guess at 50-something a little extra middle is to be expected,* she rationalized.

Fifty-something? Was she really 50-something? Others found it hard to believe. *She* found it hard to believe. She had held together fairly well over the years, and she thought and felt like a girl of 25. Wasn't it just a short time ago, though, that she was suffering through high school? Wanting desperately to fit in with the "in" crowd, the popular kids? She hadn't had the money, the attitude, or the nerve for it...only the desire...so eventually she simply accepted the fact that she would never be one of them and focused on her plans after graduation. She would go to the technical school, study "secretarial science," (what a silly name,) get a job as a legal secretary...and she hadn't thought past that. Then she met Stephen in her senior year. They were engaged five months later, married a year after that, and she followed his life. It was a good life and she was happy. She loved him so much. She hated cheating him out of so much in life, though. Of course, he insisted that she hadn't cheated him out of anything, but she knew better. It was so like him to smooth things over to spare her feelings, but she knew her irrational fears had hindered full enjoyment of their life together...for both of them.

It was a three-hour drive to the airport, and Holly thought they'd never arrive. Then suddenly the tower was in sight, and Holly's stomach did a flip-flop. As they neared the airport entrance, the nervous tics began...the smoothing of the already-smooth black sweater, the picking of microscopic pieces of lint from the red and black tiny-checked pants, the last combing of the shoulder-length dark brown straight hair, checking the teeth for signs of dark rose lipstick.

Stephen Monroe steered the SUV to the curb, parked, opened the hatch, took out her lone suitcase while she clutched the red purse and small carry-on, and she and her family said their goodbyes. "I wish you could all go inside with me," she pouted.

"Me, too," Stephen said as he hugged her tightly, his 6'2" body swallowing her small frame that was half a foot shorter. There was tension in his voice and she knew it was because he wanted to accompany her inside the terminal just to be sure everything went smoothly. She brushed his sandy hair off his face.

"I'll be fine," she whispered in his ear then kissed his cheek. "I have to do this."

"I know," he whispered back.

"Enough public displays of affection!" Holly's daughter, Rose Bowdon, scowled, pretending to be disgusted.

"Yeah, gross!" Rose's husband, Michael, agreed loudly. "Cut the PDA's!"

Keith added a vehement, "Yuck! Save it!" Holly laughed out loud at her brother's outburst.

There were hugs and kisses all around, and, of course, she had tuned up a little (her mother's term for crying) after earlier promising herself–and her family–that she wouldn't. The last time she flew, anyone and everyone could go inside the terminal. In their early years of marriage, Holly and Stephen used to go to the airport in Atlanta just to watch the planes take off and land. The events of 9/11 had changed all that.

Holly watched them climb back into the SUV, each one turning around at different times to get a last look at her. Probably to see if she was crying. She wasn't. She was glad she was able to fight back the tears. They waved as they pulled away from the curb, her son, Keith, giving her the thumbs up from the front passenger seat. *Poor thing*, Holly thought. *He usually gets stuck sitting in the back. Some day there'll be a wife by his side, though.* She smiled and waved back then picked up her carry-on and entered the terminal.

She had arrived ahead of schedule, so she was relatively relaxed as she checked her baggage and passed all the security precautions. It had really helped that Stephen had printed out her boarding pass on their home computer before leaving for the airport.

She found a seat and plopped down. She examined her nails, touched up her lipstick, checked her ticket...again... studied the crowd, smoothed her clothes, slid off her shoes, slid them back on, crossed her legs; and finally, when she realized she was fidgeting, she blew out a long breath and relaxed, at least for the moment. She would repeat most of those nervous actions more than once before boarding the plane.

Flight after flight was announced on the public address system. At first she jumped whenever an announcement was made, but after awhile she seemed to settle down. At long last her flight number was called. She jumped again then huffed in disgust at her own edginess. She inhaled deeply then slowly blew out the long breath.

Well, Holly, old gal, there's no turning back now, she thought as her stomach flip-flopped again. She rose slowly, picked up her purse and carry-on, and took her place in the line that was forming to board the 767 bound for Amsterdam, grateful she was able to find a daytime flight. She wasn't ready to fly into the night yet.

The line seemed to move at a snail's pace. *At this rate the tulips and cheese will be compost before I get there!* she griped silently. Holly just wanted to get the initial flight over with. She'd worry about the return flight later.

Her mind drifted back 3o+ years to her first flight. She could see it as if it were last week. She was 17 years old and had never been more than 200 miles from home, even by car. So flying all the way to Dallas to spend Thanksgiving with a friend had been a big deal to her and she'd been so excited! She had never been west of Georgia and always thought of "out west" as exotic, probably due to the influence of all the westerns from her childhood: *Gunsmoke, The Rifleman, Have Gun--Will Travel, Laramie, Bonanza, Rawhide,* a seemingly endless list, and she loved them all. The scenery was nothing like Georgia's. There were tumbleweeds and flat, dusty deserts, and coyotes, and mesas. It all seemed so beautiful and mysterious to her, but she had no reason to believe that she'd ever see "out west" or any of the other places from her favorite books and TV shows.

Dallas, Texas, hadn't looked that different from Georgia, but she'd had a good time anyway, never realizing that in a few years she'd see more of the west...and the north and the south and the east...than she ever could have dreamed possible...because of Stephen...a man who loved her more than life itself. He seemed to make it his life's goal to see to it that at least some of her dreams came true.

Finally, she thought, as she actually stepped onto the plane. She found her seat, an aisle seat, dropped her purse into it, and lifted her black carry-on into the overhead compartment. Thankfully it had a door that closed over it. A faint smile crossed her lips as she remembered all the trips she and Stephen had chaperoned on the high school band bus with their son and daughter.

All those trips to out-of-town football games...I wish we'd had doors to cover our belongings back then. One jolt of the brakes...those loud air brakes...then books, snacks, purses, and everything else flew into the seats and aisles, she remembered quietly. *So long ago,* she thought. She wondered where her son, daughter, son-in-law, and husband were right now. No one occupied the seat next to her yet, so she peered out the window, straining to spot them or their red SUV.

How silly! she scolded herself. *They're probably at the mall by now.* She remembered faking a pout when Rose suggested the family go shopping after they dropped Holly off. Rose's husband's groan, however, had not been faked. Michael loathed even the sight of a mall, but, good-natured soul that he was, he agreed to go.

Holly nervously took her seat and laid her head back, trying to relax. She watched the people as they boarded... a businessman checking the time on his Rolex, briefcase in hand, a teenager with a backpack and an MP3 player already plugged into one ear, a couple looking way too much in love. *Must be on their honeymoon,* she thought, her mouth breaking into a slight grin as she noticed the shiny new wedding rings.

Her mind drifted back to her honeymoon. A trip to Daytona Beach when it was in its prime. It rained all week until the day they left for home, but she was determined to play in the water anyway and came home with a cold. On the boardwalk she had fallen in love with chocolate-and-nut-covered frozen bananas, and she and Stephen had played arcade games and won a big glass casserole dish with a big glass cover that had cooked many Sunday beef roasts. They still had that dish and used it often.

Holly watched as the steady stream of passengers came onboard. An elderly lady took the seat across the aisle from her. *Somebody's grandmother,* she thought. She noticed Grandma's white canvas carry-on. "Going to Grandson's," the perfect baby blue stitching read. *Ha, that's a different one,* she giggled to herself. Several people ambled by with their bags, shoved them into the compartments and took their seats behind her. *Ah, leg room,* she sighed, as she stretched her legs. She was glad now that Stephen had insisted on buying her that first-class ticket. Of course, she had argued that there was no need for that. She had never had one before, and she didn't need one now. But he had sweetly insisted.

God, why did you give him to me? What did I ever do to deserve someone as wonderful as he is? she thought as she stared out the window, watching a food service truck drive by in one direction and a baggage carrier in another. She paused and remembered that God gives us gifts because He loves us, not because we have to earn them. She smiled and breathed heavily. In a few minutes the plane would be lifting off the runway. What would it be like after all these years? She shivered a little at the thought.

The last time she had flown was more than 25 years ago... she thought back to the trip to Washington, D.C., with her husband. Stephen was retired now and owned a successful home security system business, but when he worked with the Georgia Bureau of Investigation, he sometimes went to the nation's capital for meetings with legislators, some of whom she had met briefly. She had enjoyed that. A little girl born in a mill village in north Georgia doesn't hope to achieve such lofty goals. She had been given no reason to hope for more than a thankless job at a hometown factory and barely making ends meet. Holly had assumed early on that there would never be money for luxuries, like traveling. Life had surely turned out different than she had ever expected or imagined. *Now to Him Who is able to do exceedingly, abundantly above all that we ask or think...* She loved that verse in Ephesians.

Remembering the flight to Washington reminded her of flying over the frozen Potomac that February, which reminded her of the news reports years later of a plane crashing into the Potomac. What happened to that man who had saved so many people yet couldn't save himself? Some had said he was an angel, and that was certainly possible. She shivered, closed her eyes hard, swallowed even harder, and sighed. She checked the back of the seat in front of her. Yep, the barf bag was there.

Two girls, one blonde and one brunette, probably in their early twenties, took the two seats in front of her. They carried MP3 players as well and would probably plug them into their ears soon. *Was I ever 20?* she thought. *Yeah, and you'd already been married a whole year!* she laughed to herself. Recently someone had asked her if she'd do it all over again. She had said she would...and, *yes,* she would. She had wanted four children, two boys and two girls, by the time she was 25. Her mother was 36 years old when Holly was born, the last of three children, her brother and sister being years older than she. Although she loved her parents with all her heart, they had seemed so old as she was growing up, and her mother had some health problems during Holly's adolescent and teen years. It had not been the happiest of times, but she knew it could have been a lot worse. She wanted her children to always remember her as young and healthy and fun, hence the dream of having all her children by the age of 25.

Well, that one hadn't gone quite as she had dreamed... Rose was born when Holly was 28 and Keith at 32, and with the last pregnancy she had decided that her quiver was full. Age starts to tell on you when you are pregnant and in your 30's, especially if there is an undetected congenital blood disease involved. Five years later when it was diagnosed it was called Thalassemia minor...an overinflated name for a disease that just means the bearer is very anemic and there's nothing that can be done for it. The doctor had said something about lacking a component in the blood that processes iron.

"Go home and throw your iron pills away," the diagnostician had said. "There's nothing that will help it. Just learn to live with it." Okay. It hadn't been hard. She had lived with it all her life anyway, so nothing was really different except that now it had a name. Later genealogy research would suggest that it was inherited from an ancestor of a mixed race, maybe Cherokee and Caucasian, maybe even Cherokee and Jew. She liked that idea. Her family doctor asked if she had ancestry from Mesopotamia. Well, let's see, genius... there's Adam and Noah and Moses. She would probably never know where it had originated. Nor did it matter. Her blood would never be able to hold onto its intake of iron, no matter what she did, but that was okay. Really, she was generally apathetic about the whole subject anyway.

She kept watching the faces as they boarded the plane. A hippie–a relic from the '60's–complete with tie-dyed shirt and bell bottoms, a priest, a rabbi...she choked back a smile as she thought of all the jokes she'd heard over the years. Red Skelton, Joey Bishop, Dean Martin, Bob Hope, all the greats told a priest and rabbi joke. *I miss those guys.* And Lucille Ball...she missed Lucy, too. She did love Lucy.

Then a slender youngish man in jeans and a faded gray t-shirt stepped onto the plane. He held his head down almost shyly, but there was something familiar about him. She looked past him, still watching the passengers, then it hit her and she did a double-take. This can not be! Christopher Lapp? Chris Lapp? THE Chris Lapp? He was wearing sunglasses and a black bill cap that covered all his chestnut brown hair except for one wisp that peeked out over his right ear, but she'd know those cheekbones anywhere. *If you were trying to hide from me, buddy, you should have worn a ski mask!* she thought smugly. Thankfully, she kept her composure and looked away. No way was she going to make a fool of herself in front of Chris Lapp, the actor she admired most in the world. Yes, he was handsome, but his talent was by far his greatest asset. She had seen so many of his movies... over...and over...and over again and owned many of them on DVD. His range covered the spectrum, not only in his acting ability, but he could imitate so many different voices and accents. He truly was a gifted actor.

He checked his ticket again for the seat number and looked at her. Miraculously she was able to keep her composure. Inside, she was jelly. *Omigosh!* her brain was screaming. *His seat is next to mine!* Chris Lapp smiled at her and opened the overhead door, stuffed his black carry-on inside, and looked back at her. She pretended she didn't recognize him and smiled back.

"Excuse me," he said shyly. "I have A2. Is it okay if I step over?"

"Sure," she said, and moved her legs back as he stepped to his seat. She remembered vividly her conversation with Stephen about his purchase of a first-class ticket and how she had balked at it. *Note to self,* she now thought as she remembered her size nine shoes. *Be submissive to husband.*

She glanced down at her red open-toed shoes, grateful that they were clean and her toenails were neatly polished with a matching red. *Thank you, God.* It amused her to think that only a woman would care about the condition of her feet in the presence of a celebrity!

He was well known...not a megastar...yet...but he was on his way, and she knew he had the potential. He was definitely "A-list" material. Maybe that was one of the reasons she liked him more than all the others...because she saw his ability to pull off practically any role. She reached for her purse pretending to search for something, unwilling to be like all the other fans and fawn all over him. How tasteless. He had to be sick of that. *I might have been born in the mill village, but my mama taught me manners,* she thought to herself. Holly also wasn't going to invade his privacy by striking up a conversation with him. Her faux purse inventory was over, so she set it back down on the floor at her feet. She thought she was still watching the people board the plane but soon realized that she was watching Chris in her peripheral vision. He was holding a small black portfolio in his lap and looking out the window. She could tell that he looked over at her once for a couple of seconds then looked back out the window. What was that all about? "You're being paranoid," she spoke sharply to herself under her breath.

There were so many emotions invading her brain...and her breathing...right now that she wasn't sure how she was going to handle this trip at all. It was hard to get a deep breath. She squirmed a little, trying not to be obvious that she was struggling to breathe. She leaned forward and finally caught a good deep one and let it out slowly, not wanting to draw attention to herself. Sighing dyspnea. That's what the family allergist had called it once. Sometimes caused by stress. She didn't pretend to understand all that.

Holly relaxed a little and sat back. Her peripheral vision told her Chris was still looking out the window and had not seemed to notice. *Please don't let me have a panic attack! Not here! Not now!*

The flight attendants took their places and announced the required flight instructions, but Holly didn't hear a word of it. She was concentrating on keeping her composure.

"Ping." The "Fasten Seatbelts" directive came from the lighted sign on the ceiling in front of her. She and Chris obeyed. The plane slowly began to taxi down the runway and she felt her fingers tense and clench into fists in her lap. She breathed in and out slowly and calmly. *God, please be with me,* she prayed silently. *Help me trust You.* They waited for two planes ahead of them to receive clearance for takeoff. She watched them soar into the clouds and knew her plane was next. She swallowed hard. The plane started down the runway, gaining speed with every second. She could hear the jet engines whine and the sound grew more shrill with every moment that passed. She tried to appear calm by putting her arms on the armrests and letting her fingers hang off the edges. At least she *looked* relaxed. She could tell they were climbing higher, but she dared not look past Chris and out the window. After awhile she could tell they had leveled off.

"This is Captain Miller. I'll be taking you to Amsterdam today. We are cruising at 600 miles per hour and 34,000 feet. The air temperature is 70 degrees Fahrenheit, 21 degrees Celsius in Amsterdam, where it's mostly cloudy. We should be arriving at Schiphol Airport in approximately eight hours."

34,000 feet...well, **now** *I'm comforted,* she sarcastically thought, closing her eyes. *I need a distraction.* She glanced quickly at Chris and saw that he was looking around, first out the window, then straight ahead, then around the cabin. *I will NOT make him talk to me!* She gritted her teeth and looked straight ahead.

"Do you get as bored as I do on these long flights?" He was speaking to *her!*

Oh, God, please help me with this answer, she pleaded silently. How in the world was she going to answer this without looking like a first-class idiot? First class. Cute, but no pun intended. She looked at him, and he was smiling as he awaited her sure-to-be foolish answer. "Well, actually," she began, carefully choosing her words, "I haven't flown in 27 years." She just knew he'd think she was a dull homebody and eventually turn back toward the window to silently ride out the remainder of the flight in misery and boredom. Boy, did he get the wrong traveling companion.

"Really?" he asked, eyebrows raised.

"Really," she answered, rolling her eyes. "Disgusting, huh?" she asked. *Oh, boy,* she thought. She just knew he was thinking, *What a loser!*

Instead, he said, "Not at all. Some travel a lot and some don't. Takes all kinds to make a world." He smiled and turned back toward the window.

Thank you, God, she smiled to herself. He was opening his portfolio now and taking out a pencil. The portfolio contained what appeared to be a sketch pad. He sat for a moment looking forward, then he started drawing something on the clean white paper. *I will not watch, I will not watch, I will not watch,* she said to herself, looking straight ahead. The repetition reminded her of the time in eighth grade when her teacher had made her write 500 times, "I will not talk while the teacher is talking." It had taken forever, but she had finished it and turned it in like the compliant child that she was. Could she help it that she had been an outgoing child, talking whenever she wanted, whether the teacher was or not?

Her peripheral vision told her that Chris was drawing in great detail, taking his time with whatever it was he was sketching. All of a sudden the plane dipped slightly, and she sucked in a breath. *Oh, no,* she thought, tucking her chin and looking over to see if Chris had heard her. Apparently not... he was erasing a wrong turn his pencil had taken as a result of the jolt. She glanced toward Grandma to see if she had heard her. Nope, she had fallen asleep quickly and had slept right through it. *Must be nice,* Holly scowled. The plane took another sudden dip and corrected quickly. *This is just too much!* she thought, beginning to feel the panic rise in her chest.

Her thoughts went back to the last plane ride she had taken, the one coming back to Atlanta from Washington, D.C. Nothing really had happened except that the plane had run into light turbulence and bounced like a car riding down a freshly cut dirt road full of large holes. That's fine for dirt roads but not for the friendly skies, and it had been frightening to a person who had been spoiled by smooth flights. She had decided then and there never to fly again. Had something happened to her early in her life that had put so much fear in her? There was just no reason to be that afraid. She had the same fear of roller coasters. She had been on those, too. And she hated them. It must have something to do with not being in control. After all, her fear of heights was not so bad. It was there, just not that great. Her fear of riding in elevators had calmed tremendously from what it had been in years past. That was what had prompted her to take this "test flight" to The Netherlands. Things seemed to be looking up in the fear department, so why not give flying another try?

Why in the world did I decide to take such a long flight? And over water, no less? Why didn't I choose to take a little thirty-minute trip to test myself? Why didn't I listen to all my friends and family who told me to start out slowly? Holly was beating herself up with questions. She was beginning to feel her insides quiver.

No! No! Please, God, don't let me panic! Please don't let me cry! It was too late. Her hands were now shaking, too, and pretty soon Chris would notice and she would be mortified. She was fighting to keep her hands still. The tears were welling up in her eyes, and she put her shaking hands to each side of her face to hide her eyes from Chris and Grandma. She reached for her purse with her left hand. During her pretend inventory of its contents she seemed to remember seeing a pocket pack of tissues. Sure enough, with her left eye exposed now Chris noticed.

"Are you okay?" he asked, the concern showing in his furrowed brow. He was still wearing his sunglasses, but she knew the look in his eyes. She'd seen it a hundred times in his movies.

"Um." Her voice quivered. "No, I'm not, actually" she managed to say with embarrassment. She found the tissues and plucked one from the package and dabbed at her eyes trying not to smear her mascara. *My makeup must be a mess now,* she thought. *I bet I look like a raccoon.*

"Is there anything I can do for you?" he whispered, leaning forward a little. He seemed to sense her embarrassment.

"I don't think so," she whispered back. "Just please don't make fun of me."

"I'd never do that...especially since I don't know what I'd be making fun of you for," he teased with a smile. She was still shaking.

"The reason I haven't flown in 27 years is that I developed a fear of flying back then. I'm so sorry to do this to you." She was feeling a sob welling up in her throat but managed to push it back down. This was terrible. Not only was she miserable, but now she was making the flight miserable for her seat mate, not to mention that her seat mate was Chris Lapp! *Good job, Holly.* She sensed a long, agonizing flight...for both of them.

He patted her arm. "You're not doing anything to me. I'm just sorry this is happening to you. I feel kinda helpless," was his sympathetic response.

"I feel like everyone is watching me," she said, turning her body a little toward him just in case others were looking. At least they wouldn't be able to see her face so well then.

He looked around. "No, no one is looking at all. It's just me, and I'm not making fun of you. I'll help you if you'll tell me what I can do."

"There's nothing you can do," she said. Recent reads had put to flight any notion that Chris Lapp was a Christian, so asking him to pray was out of the question. The plane gave another little jolt and corrected again. She jumped slightly and looked over at him, embarrassed. "I'm so sorry," she whispered.

"It really *is* all right," he whispered back. She nervously crossed her arms and squeezed opposite biceps tightly. She wanted desperately to rock back and forth but knew that would quickly draw attention, so she just froze and breathed hard. *We've only been in the air, what, 45 minutes...what am I going to do for another eight hours?!* she wondered.

Chris sensed the need to distract her. "Where do you live?" he asked, hoping it would make her mind stray from the problem at hand. Then, "No, let me guess. Judging from your lovely accent I'd say either Alabama or Georgia." He gave her a questioning look. "Right?

"Wells, Georgia," she answered, her voice quivering. "It's in the southern part of the state." She was still shaking. "I'm so sorry," she apologized again. "I thought I could do this." She was grateful that no one else seemed to have recognized him. The scene might have been quite embarrassing, people coming to him for autographs and finding her crying. Fodder for the tabloids for sure. She could see the headlines now: Chris Lapp Brings Traveling Companion to Tears, Chris Lapp Terrorizes Woman on Plane, Chris Lapp and New Lady Friend Feud in the Skies, Chris Lapp and Alien Woman Battle over First Class Seat, Alien Woman's Tears Heal Chris Lapp of Mystery Disease. Yikes.

"You can," he promised. "I'll help you, if I can."

The plane suddenly took a dip, a longer one this time before it corrected. She jerked and he reacted and grabbed both her hands. She squeezed them hard, grateful for human touch. She realized she was squeezing so hard that she might be hurting him, remembering her last flight with her husband when she held his arm so tightly that she left fingernail prints in it. She loosened her grip. *God, please calm me down. I'm making a fool of myself,* she desperately prayed. *Yea, though I walk through the valley of the shadow of death, I will fear no evil.* Oddly enough, she almost laughed. She was hardly dying...but there was something about Psalm 23 that always comforted her. *Jesus, please help me.* At that moment, a peace came over her, she let go of Chris's hands, and let out a slow breath. That old song was still right...Jesus, There's Just Something about that Name.

"You look better," he said, noticing her tension subside.

"I feel better," she said calmly. She had stopped shaking. "Look, the color is coming back to your hands," she quietly joked. He looked down and laughed. "I'm so sorry," she apologized.

"No need to apologize. It's okay, really," he insisted. Under the false impression that she still needed to be distracted, he said, "Let's start this conversation again. Hi. I'm Chris." He extended his hand.

Although surprised he gave his real name, she shook his hand and said, "I'm Holly." After the "nice to meet yous," he began calmly asking her about Wells, her family, her life. She told him about acres and acres of cotton and soybeans and watermelons and peanuts, of famous people who lived in the area, of her wonderful husband, her daughter, son-in-law, and son, all the while being very careful not to question him about his life. After awhile she began to feel selfish for not appearing to care about his life and constantly talking about hers, but she didn't want to put him on the spot, forcing him to tell her that he was a famous movie star. She wanted this time to stay pure and uncomplicated. After all, this was a once-in-a-lifetime blessing for her, and she didn't want to squander it. She hoped she could be a blessing to him, too, and maybe allow him to have a hassle-free flight for once. *Oh, well,* she thought matter-of-factly. *Too late for that, I guess.* She smiled and said, "Well, I guess this is one long flight that's not gonna be too boring for you."

He smiled and nodded then said, "So far it's been quite interesting." They both laughed.

There was a lull in the conversation, so she laid her head back, tired from all the tension, but fighting sleep. What would she tell her family and friends when they found out she had flown with Chris Lapp and asked what it was like? "Oh, I slept most of the time!" But sleep she did, albeit for only an hour.

She opened her eyes, realizing that she had been asleep for awhile. Her fear was that she had snored or drooled. Chris was sleeping, his portfolio closed and tucked beside him. *Good,* she thought. *Maybe he slept through anything unladylike that I might have done.* She glanced over at Grandma. Still asleep. Instinctively, she watched to see if she was still breathing, something she had done with her children from the time they were born. "Yep, still going," she thought as she watched Grandma's chest rise and fall. She looked back at Chris and saw that he was awake now.

"Looks like we both needed a rest," he said.

"Looks that way," she agreed, putting her hand over her mouth as she yawned.

"You seem so relaxed now," he said with a puzzled look on his face. "And I don't think it's from the nap."

"Let's just say I prayed hard," she said with a knowing look. "Hmm," he said thoughtfully and opened his mouth to speak but just then the flight attendant appeared in the aisle with drinks and snacks.

"What would you like?" She was very pleasant and spoke perfect English with a beautiful French accent.

"Just orange juice for me," she said.

"And me," Chris echoed. "Oh, uh, you wouldn't happen to have any almonds, would you?"

"As a matter of fact, I do," she said with a perky smile.

"Me, too," said Holly.

After proper "thank-yous" he continued his skeptical thoughts aloud. "Well,...I don't know about that. Prayer, I mean."

"What don't you know about prayer?" she asked. He simply laughed. She smiled and said, "No, really, what do you mean?"

He hesitated a moment then said, "I'm not sure I believe in all that stuff about God and prayer."

"Why wouldn't you believe it? Why is that hard for you?" she questioned, a look of concern forming on her brow.

"I don't know...I guess it's just the way I was raised. We didn't go to church much...occasionally on Easter or at Christmas, I guess. And maybe a few times in between."

She took a sip of her juice. It bought her time to pray silently. *Okay, You and me, God. Please tell me what to say.* She swallowed, set her cup down, and opened her package of almonds. "You know, going to church doesn't have anything to do with being a Christian or praying or any of that stuff."

He looked a little confused as he chewed. "Huh?"

"You don't earn God's favor. You can't buy His love or attention by doing good things like going to church or giving money to the poor. That's a trap people have fallen into because human love isn't always unconditional. In fact, it's rarely unconditional. But God's *is*."

He thought a minute then said, "I thought you had to be good and not tell too many lies and not cheat on your income tax and not do a lot of bad stuff, you know?"

"I know, I know...been there, done that," she came back quickly.

"Well, anyway," he shrugged, "I've not been a very good boy for, lo, these many years," he quipped. "He's not interested in me anyway."

"Nothing could be further from the truth," she said, looking straight into his eyes. She looked away for a second, took a deep breath, then looked back into his eyes. "What do you think you have to do to be 'good enough' for God?"

"Well, like I said, don't tell too many lies and..."

She cut him off with, "And how many is too many?"

He thought a moment then laughed and said, "I haven't the foggiest."

She laughed and said, "You've heard of The Ten Commandments?" He gave her a sarcastic smile and said, "Yessss.."

"Well, do you know that if you tell one lie or misuse God's name just one time or break any of the others just once, you've broken them all?"

"How is that?" he asked, completely confused now.

"Well," she answered, "God's standard is perfection, and no one has ever lived a perfect life...except Jesus Christ. Ever heard of Him?" He gave her the sarcastic smile again. "Know Who He is?" she asked him.

"I've heard," he retorted.

"Then you probably know that He is God's only Son and that God sent Him to die for our sins. And we all sin, whether we like to admit it or not. I know it's something you're probably not comfortable talking about. Believe me, there was a time when I wasn't either. It was hard for me to even say His Name! Jesus!" She laughed. "You want to hear my story?" He looked somewhat interested now.

"Sure. I'm all ears. Anyway, you have a captive audience! I'm not going anywhere!" he said, waving his hand around in front of them.

"Oh, I wouldn't force my story on you! All you have to do is tell me you want to talk about something else and that's what we'll do," she said, sensing she had gotten his attention and he wasn't about to let her talk about anything else.

"Nothing doing," he said, settling back, his eyes taking direct aim at hers.

"Okay, well, I was brought up in a family that went to church almost every Sunday. You didn't ask on Saturday night whether we were going to church the next day...it was just understood that we were, you know?" He nodded. His eyes seemed far away for a moment. Then he looked back at her. "Well, to make a long story shorter, I was in church most of my life but never really got a whole lot out of what was said. Don't ask me why, I just didn't. Maybe I wasn't paying attention or something, I don't know. Anyway, when I was about 30 years old, this lady that I sang in the choir with at church...I still went to church..." she rolled her eyes and shook her head. "This lady kept inviting me to come to a Bible study. Of course, the last thing I wanted to do was go to a Bible study, so every time she invited me, I always came up with an excuse. One day she caught me off guard, and I promised her I'd go. I thought that if I went this one time maybe she'd shut up and leave me alone about it."

He laughed and said, "Yeah, I know."

"Has that happened to you?" she asked, wrinkling her brow. "Well, sorta," he said, losing his smile. He recovered quickly and said, "Hey, this is your story, remember?"

She laughed and said, "Oh, yeah." She knew there was a story behind what he had said. Maybe he would tell her about it later.

"Anyway, I went to the Bible study, and believe it or not, they were talking that very day about how much God loves us and about not being right with God and how you could go about correcting that. Well, I knew that I wasn't right with God...that there was sin in my life and that I was just sorta living it out not knowing how or where I was going to end up. I knew that wasn't right, and the plan was laid out there right in front of me in the study book they were using, with a place to sign and date it and everything. For me, personally, it was like a business transaction, but everyone's story is different."

"What do you mean? What was 'laid out' for you?" he asked, with a puzzled look.

"The plan that would set me free, give me peace, put me right with God, set my life's course out before me," she said with a smile. "See, everybody's different. God knows that. He made us, so nothing's a surprise to Him. Nothing. Not even the fact that you haven't been such a good boy for a long time," she teased. He smiled. "That's called sin," she said and took another sip of her juice.

God, please open his heart now to hear and accept what You're about to say to him, she took the opportunity for silent prayer again.

"And the Bible says that sin separates us from God, Who created us. The creator of anything doesn't want to be separated from his creation. And the fact is that without atonement we're separated from God forever. See there's Heaven and there's Hell, and whether folks want to believe that or not, they are real places."

A look of disgust fell on his face, and she threw both her hands up in the air, tilted her head, and said, "I know, I know. I'd rather overlook that myself, but it's true."

He was thoughtful for a moment then asked, "So what brings a *sinner*," he emphasized the word and rolled his eyes, "back together with God?"

"Well," she said, "the Bible says that to atone for sin there must be a blood sacrifice. That's the reason for all the animal sacrifices in the Old Testament...you know, bulls and birds and lambs...always from spotless animals, animals without blemish or imperfection. Well, God promised a new covenant that wouldn't involve sacrifice after sacrifice. There would be one sacrifice, and that would be it. Turns out that was His perfect Son, Jesus Christ...a lamb without spot or blemish. That's the reason He's sometimes referred to as 'The Lamb of God.' The reason He was born was to die for us that one sacrifice. So the plan is that you acknowledge that you're a sinner, and it doesn't matter how LONG one has been a sinner," she said, giving him a sarcastic grin, "tell God you know you're a sinner, be truly sorry and tell Him so, ask His forgiveness, and tell Him that you want to accept Jesus as that payment for your sins and move on with Him from then on." She stopped talking and gave him time to think and maybe ask questions. He didn't for a long time.

Then he said, "I don't know about all that. I've lived this way for a long time."

Her voice grew softer and slower as she said, "Are you happy with that life? If you died suddenly, are you certain of where you'd go?" Just then the plane jolted again. She laughed at God's timing. Chris looked surprised then thought a second and laughed out loud.

In a moment he asked, "A short time ago you would have been trembling...now you're laughing?"

"I know...ain't God good?" She beamed as she looked past Chris out the window of an airplane for the first time in 27 years.

CHAPTER TWO

Chris smiled and turned toward the window. He didn't move for a long while and was unusually quiet. She wondered if she had said something that struck a nerve, made him angry, upset him in some other way. Whatever the situation, she knew she had done the right thing...she had such a peace about their conversation. She glanced over at him a couple of times but didn't want to interrupt his thoughts, whatever they were, so she took out the book she had brought along, just in case the trip was boring. Laughable thought now.

She looked at her watch and realized that, if the flight was on time, they only had a couple of hours more until they landed in Amsterdam, and it was sad to think that this rare opportunity was almost over. She had experienced so many emotions and feelings... concern, surprise, anxiety, fear, anticipation, elation, peace...but her one concern was whether she had made a difference in his life with her testimony. She may never know, and by the looks of things, they may never talk again. She glanced at Chris again. He was looking down, deep in thought. Holly hoped he was considering seriously their conversation about Jesus. She knew his peripheral vision would betray her, so she looked back at her book and opened it...but soon realized she wasn't reading, just staring at the page. Shaking her thoughts loose and trying to concentrate on reading, she had finished only two pages when Chris asked, "What're you reading?"

"Oh," she said, returning to reality, "a book about the great comics of the '50's and '60's. You know, Martin and Lewis, Lucy and Desi, George and Gracie, Jack Benny, Red Skelton, Carol Burnett. I figured I'd bring along something light and funny since I wasn't sure how rough this flight was going to be, if you get my drift." She turned her head sideways and rolled her eyes.

"And how has it been?" he asked, smiling.

"Not as I expected, actually," she answered, not elaborating on what she really meant. Little did he know! "Although, I'm not sure exactly what I expected it to be like." She wrinkled her brow in thought then turned to him and added, "You were certainly a big help, and I really appreciate it. You know, you could have just ignored me completely."

He looked shocked. "Are you serious? How rude would that have been!"

She laughed and said, "Well, as you say, 'It takes all kinds to make a world,' and some are not as nice as you are."

He gave her his "Aw, g'won" face (she'd seen that one a hundred times, too) and asked to look at the book. She handed it to him, and he flipped to the jacket and read about the author. "Well, she should know," he said. "She was there." Then he flipped through a couple of pages and scanned some of the great old pictures of the adored entertainers. She wondered if he realized he had slipped up with that last comment. If she asked him what he meant by, "she was there," he would have to admit to being a celebrity, so she ignored it. The author was not well known by the general public but had been on the inside track during the heyday of the greats, even personal assistant to a couple of them, according to her bio. Only someone on the inside track himself would know that.

"I love these guys," he said shaking his head. "Too bad their day is over."

"Yeah," she said. "There are plenty of funny guys around now, but none of them have what the oldies had, whatever that was. And I don't care for the off-color jokes of today's comedians. Besides the fact that it displeases God, it's distracting."

"Pretty safe to say, then, that you won't be taking in a comedy show in Amsterdam, huh?" he asked with a laugh, handing the book back to her.

"Not if I can avoid it!" she came back.

"What will you be doing while you're there?" he asked.

"Well-l-l," she drawled, "I hadn't really given it too much thought because I was mainly focusing on the flight over. To tell you the truth, I was afraid the trip would be so bad that I'd hole up in my hotel room dreading the trip home!" He snickered then she continued, "The trip was so good that now I'm looking forward to my couple of days in Amsterdam. Guess I need to figure out something to do."

"Couple of days?!" he asked in disbelief. "Just a couple of days?"

She said, "Yeah, well, this was only a test trip...you know, to see if I could take flying again."

"And you attempted it alone? And a trip this long? Wow, I think you're a stronger person than you think you are!" he said, pointing a finger at her. She pretended not to notice the familiar star tattoo on his index finger that she'd seen in so many pictures.

"Yeah, well," she said sheepishly, "I haven't made it back home yet."

He grinned. "You'll do fine. Maybe you won't have a seat mate who jabbers away and you'll get that book read on your flight back."

"Oh, please," she said, "You haven't jabbered away. In fact, I think God put you here to help me get through this flight. I hope He gives me someone like you to help pass the time on the return flight."

He nodded and said, "Maybe so." They were quiet for a few minutes, and she asked if he'd ever been to The Netherlands before, to which he answered that he'd been there three or four times "on business." Of course, she didn't ask what kind of business. Instead she began to think aloud about possible activities during her brief stay.

"One of the reasons I chose to come to The Netherlands on my test trip was because I love tulips. They're my favorite flower, and they're blooming now...*en masse*, I hear. I can't wait to see them. When I was a little girl, my daddy teased me for constantly keeping my nose in a book. I read books with pictures of big fields of tulips blooming in The Netherlands. Acres and acres. Ever since then I've wanted to see them. There's a place about an hour from Amsterdam, near Lisse, that I'm thinking of taking a cab to see, if I can."

"So you're a bookworm?" he questioned.

"Oh, yeah, and since my children are grown, I have more time to read than I used to," she said. "My time then was taken with school activities, sports, band and choir stuff, and church activities, but I loved it. Now that they're grown, I'm not so busy any more, so I have more time to read and do other things...like run off to Europe by myself!"

She grinned, and he said, "You just might join the jet set, huh?" and laughed aloud.

"Not likely," she disagreed with a grin. "If I get used to this flying thing again, I would want to travel A LOT, and that takes tons of money. My husband makes a great living, but I have an addictive personality. I'd spend way too much money traveling."

"Well," he said, looking thoughtful, "maybe your family knows some people who have private places that they would let you use?" he asked, trying to be helpful. "That would cut the cost."

"Nah, not really. Maybe a few in Florida, but not really anywhere else," she answered. "No big deal." She was uncomfortable with the conversation, knowing that he had lots of money, so she steered the discussion back to her agenda in The Netherlands. "Another reason I chose The Netherlands is cheese."

He looked at her quizzically. "Excuse me? Cheese?"

She laughed and said, "Yeah, cheese. I love cheese, well, actually, I just love food!" She giggled then said, "I wanted to eat some of the cheese that The Netherlands is known for...you know, gouda and Leerdammer and Edam and, well, I don't know what other kinds, but I guess I'll find out." She hesitated, then added, "And when I do, I'll eat 'em!" She waited for him to get the joke.

He winced and said, "Edam? Aw, that stinks."

"Like Limberger?"

"Aw, man. That's weird, girl," he said as he shook his head and laughed. He was not nearly as formal and shy as he had been at first, and she was glad to see that he was loosening up a little. She wondered what he'd think if he found out that she knew his true identity. *Well, that'll never happen,* she thought, proud of the fact that she had kept such a secret. "Yeah, maybe I'll get a sack of cheeses, catch a cab to the tulip fields, and sit in a field of yellow tulips eating cheese! Wouldn't that be a sight? You just gotta know someone would see me and take a picture that would end up on one of those postcards in the souvenir shops!" They laughed aloud at the idea.

The conversation lulled then Chris said, "Why yellow?"

"Huh?" she asked. "Oh, you mean, why yellow tulips?"

"Yeah," he answered.

"Oh...well...yellow is my favorite color, but I like tulips of all colors. I just thought yellow tulips with yellow cheese would be a nice picture." He rolled his bottom lip out and nodded then turned toward the window and was quiet for awhile. She decided not to disturb him, just on the off chance that he was remembering their conversation about Jesus. She laid her head back on the headrest and stared at the ceiling for awhile, contemplating whether or not she had left out any important part of her testimony. She decided that she had included enough for him to chew on for awhile.

"This is Captain Miller. We're approaching Amsterdam and will be landing at Schiphol in approximately 30 minutes."

Her heart sank...the flight would be over soon, and it made her sad to think about it. But, boy, would she have a story to tell her family and friends when she returned home! And she could hardly wait to tell them! She smiled to herself and sat thinking about the events of the past few hours.

She was jolted from her reverie by Chris's voice asking, "Do you think it would be too forward of me to ask for your e-mail address? Would your husband be upset?" She couldn't believe her ears but said, "Oh, he wouldn't mind at all. And I'd like yours, too. When I tell him how I got through this flight, he'll probably want to e-mail you his gratitude himself!" They laughed as he ripped a page from his portfolio and scribbled his, tore it off and handed it and the remainder of the paper to her. She scribbled hers and handed the ragged sheet back to him. She looked at his and noticed the beginning said, "Clapptwice." She got it immediately...she knew his name was Christopher Terrence Lapp, Jr., so "Clapptwice" made perfect sense. "C" for Christopher, "lapp" for his last name and "twice" because he was a junior. Clever. "I have several e-mail addresses, but this one is ultra private, so please don't give it to anyone else," he requested, hesitantly.

She assumed he was a little fearful that she would ask him why. She didn't. Instead, assuming an air of importance she said, "Well, I only have two e-mail addresses, but this is my most private one!" to which they both laughed.

CHAPTER THREE

"Would you do me a favor?" he asked.

"Sure, what is it?" she answered, wondering what in the world he could possibly want.

"Could I get a picture with you?"

"Sure, if you want to," she answered, not believing *he* was asking for a picture with *her*. It hadn't occurred to *her* to get a picture with *him*, probably a subconscious attempt to remain low-key about his identity.

"Great. When we get inside the airport, maybe we can find someone who'll snap a quick one for me."

"Okay," she said, "on one condition." He looked confused.

"No fair. You've already promised!" he complained.

"Just kidding," she said. "I was just going to ask you to e-mail it to me. Better yet, we'll just get our photographer-at-large to take one with my camera, too. After all," she said matter-of-factly, "I had to bring it to take pictures of tulips and cheese."

He shook his head and laughed. "Of course you did."

They were instructed to fasten their seatbelts again. As Holly buckled hers, she could see the lights of Amsterdam appearing through the dusky sky as they approached the city.

She turned to him and said, "I have to admit that I'm sorry this flight is ending." She shook her head then said, "I can't believe I'm saying that because initially I was so apprehensive about the flight. You really were such a rock, though, and helped me get through it. Thank you again so much. My husband and kids are going to be so grateful. I know they're concerned about me, so I need to call them as soon as I get checked into my hotel." She paused as she remembered the looks on their faces as they drove away from her at the airport. "I hated to do this to them, but somehow I just had to find out by myself if I could do it or not."

"I understand. They're going to be very proud of you," he said confidently, taking a look out the window. When he looked back at her, he noticed her eyes were softer and shiny. "I'm sorry...I didn't mean to make you cry." He looked so apologetic that she felt sorry for him.

"Oh, forget it," she said wiping a single tear from her cheek. "This day has been so emotional for me, and I'm sort of a cry-baby anyway. I can't believe I've actually done this after 27 years!" She pressed her lips together hard...she just didn't want to cry *again*. Then she started to laugh quietly, not wanting to draw attention.

"What's so funny?" he asked, his eyes wide with surprise. "I told you I'm emotional. Sometimes I cry, sometimes I laugh, sometimes I do both! I'm just really, really happy," was her only explanation. Of course, she couldn't tell him the whole truth.

He looked at her for a long time. "You know," he said finally, "this has actually been a good flight for me, too. The best in a very long time. Maybe some day I can tell you why." She looked at him obviously confused. "Well, I do have your e-mail address, you know. So maybe some day I'll e-mail you with the explanation."

Her curiosity was aroused, but all she said was, "Then you'd better not lose it!"

He had tucked it safely away. "Don't worry," he said as he patted his shirt pocket.

"I brought my laptop, and, since it's so late, I'll probably stay in my room tonight and catch up on my e-mails. I just know my inbox is packed. I didn't really tell many people about this trip...just in case it didn't go well. Then I wouldn't have a lot of people to have to explain to, so people probably continued to e-mail me thinking I'm home. Guess now it's safe to let them know where I am. Boy, will they be surprised!" She wondered what people would say to her when she got home.

He looked thoughtful then said, "They should all be happy for you. I bet you'll get lots of 'atta girls,' and you'll deserve every one of 'em." She gave him a bashful smile and thanked him. They were quiet for a minute or two, then he asked, "When did you say you're leaving for home?"

She thought a minute and said, "I don't think I did, but my flight is Friday morning at 10:00. I should have two full days to enjoy the tulips and cheese." He smiled and nodded as she laughed and shook her head. She took out her return ticket and said, "Maybe I'd better check the time just to be sure." She scanned the information on the ticket. "Yep, 10:00 a.m., seat G1." He quickly scanned the seat numbers above their heads.

"Good," he said with an approving nod. "That's the front row...plenty of leg room...and a window seat. You'll be able to handle a window seat on your return flight, won't you?" She thought a second then nodded, "Yeah, I think I will. No, I'm SURE I will."

They could see the runway lights clearly now and felt the plane start to bank for the landing. The sky was cloudy as they approached the runway. "I've always said this is one of the best parts of a flight...landing!" she said with a laugh.

"It's also one of the most dangerous," he said then caught himself. "Oops...wrong thing to say, huh?" He gave her an apologetic grin.

"That's okay," she said. "My husband tells me the same thing. He says that the takeoff and the landing are the most dangerous parts of a flight. Still, it just feels good to know we're landing."

Chris noticed she became quiet and had a faraway look in her eyes. "Something wrong?" he asked. Holly returned to the present, looked at him sadly, and said, "For years one of Stephen's dreams was to get his pilot's license. He began lessons several years ago, when the kids were small and his mother was still alive, but when he realized that no one wanted to fly with him, he gave them up." She looked down then said, "Something else I cheated him out of."

Chris felt sorry for her and said, "Surely he doesn't blame you. It wasn't your fault that *no one* would fly with him." She quickly defended Stephen. "Oh, no, no! He never blamed me, but I did."

The wheels attacked the runway with a short screech, and the plane slowed to a crawl as it glided to the gate. They finally came to a stop and were given the okay to gather their belongings and deplane. She picked up her purse, retrieved her carry-on from the overhead compartment and moved out of Chris's way. He picked up his portfolio, opened the compartment and dragged out his backpack. They left the plane and entered the airport, searching for the baggage pickup area.

"Have you ever seen so many suitcases?" she said, her eyes wide in amazement.

"Yeah, and almost all of them black. Wonder why that is," he laughed holding up his black carry-on. She snickered and said, "I think it's because so many travelers are men, and men are afraid of color."

He smiled sarcastically and said, "Oh, yeah? And what's your excuse?" he asked pointing to her black carry-on. She raised her head snobbishly and replied, "I'm just stylish!" then walked away with her nose in the air. He watched her turn around and come back laughing. They stood watching the luggage carousel for what seemed like an eternity, then he spotted his suitcase and lifted it off the conveyor belt. "Still think men are afraid of color, missy?" he asked her as he held up the small red bag.

"Well, I must say I'm surprised," she admitted.

"I got tired of trying to figure out which of the black bags was mine after every flight, so I decided to remedy the problem a long time ago."

"I can see that," she said pointing to all the nicks in the leather. "Must have been *quite* a long time ago."

He glanced down at the scrapes and said, "Actually, it hasn't been as long as it appears. I just travel a lot." As she caught a glimpse of her suitcase rounding the curve on the carousel and picked it up, she was glad for the distraction from the conversation. She knew full well why he traveled so much. She changed the subject to the next order of business: how to get to her hotel.

"Guess I'll see if I can catch a cab to my hotel. It's only about ten miles from the airport, so maybe it won't take long to get out of here and get checked in," she said, looking around for an exit that would take her out to what she hoped would be a line of taxis.

"Well, if you don't think it too forward of me, and if our hotels are close, I would be glad to share a cab with you. You've never been here before, right?" She shook her head in the negative. He nodded and said, "Well, as I said, I've been several times, so I guess that makes me the official tour guide."

They laughed then she said, "That actually makes me feel better."

"Where are you staying?" he asked.

"My husband is a hopeless romantic and insisted that I stay at The Crimson Tulip downtown. He found it on the internet and said it sounded like me."

He smiled and said, "He sounds like quite a guy."

With a smile she said, "He is. Wouldn't surprise me to find a vase of tulips in my room...yellow ones, even if it *is* The Crimson Tulip."

He laughed and said, "You're not going to believe this, but my hotel is next door to The Crimson Tulip."

"No way! What's the name of it...The Chartreuse Lily?" she quipped.

He grimaced and said, "Not quite. It's the Hotel Adell." Just then they reached the exit, walked through and immediately spotted a cab. He hailed it, the cabby loaded their things in the trunk and asked them their destinations, in surprisingly good English. Chris told him the hotel names, and they all got in and took off.

"You don't drive like the drivers in New York City, Klaus" she said, noticing his name on the dashboard.

Klaus smiled and said, "Thank you. You're kinder than most."

Chris said, "So you have been a bit of a world traveler, huh? New York...pretty big-time place for a lady who says she hasn't been anywhere much."

She gave him a hold-your-horses look and said, "I just said I'd never traveled by plane much. I've traveled in the States a lot by car and train...San Francisco, Los Angeles, Denver, Dallas, New Orleans, New York, Miami, and lots of other places. And also Toronto."

He nodded. "I'm impressed."

She shook her head. "No need to be. I was always with my husband. Not much of a loner."

They traveled on, passing hotels and restaurants and sidewalk cafes just closing up for the night. Her supper was fading on her and she hoped to find a vending machine or an open snack shop at The Crimson Tulip. They passed a hotel with a lighted fountain that danced to music, and she was glad the traffic slowed just before they passed in front of it so she could watch the water squirt back and forth and around and around in rhythm with the music, the multicolored lights blinking at each movement of the water. "I love these things!" she giggled. "There's one in Atlanta near Olympic Park."

"Yeah, I was there in 1996 for a portion of the Olympics and saw it. Pretty cool," he said, stretching his neck to see the fountain as it disappeared from view. He turned toward the front again and said, "Our hotels should be just around the curve up ahead." After a minute or two the lights of the hotels came into view.

"I suppose mine is the one with the big red tulip over the door," she declared with a grin.

"Pretty fair assumption," he said, "and mine is the one to the right with the big green "A" on top.

"I like Amsterdam so far," she said with an approving nod. "Let's just hope they come through with the tulips and cheese."

He shook his head. "You're bent on tulips and cheese, aren't you?" he said as he gathered his things.

"Yes, sir, I am," she replied emphatically as she gathered hers.

Klaus parked in front of The Crimson Tulip, got out, opened the trunk and retrieved their bags. She and Chris slid from the back seat and she opened her purse, scrounging around for her wallet to pay her share of the cab fare.

"Put it back," he said, taking out his money clip. "I got it." Before she could object he had shoved the money into Klaus's hand and said, "Keep the change." Klaus raised his eyebrows and said a hearty, "Thank you, sir!" as he got back into the cab.

"Well, thanks," she said, "but you didn't have to do that. I thought we were splitting the fare."

"Consider it a gift," he said with a smile and a wave of his hand.

They picked up their bags and started up the walkway toward The Crimson Tulip. As they got to the doorway, Chris stopped and said, "I really had a great time. Thanks for making the long flight so enjoyable."

Her mouth dropped open, and she said, "I can't believe you said that! I was a freak! At least in the beginning!"

He laughed and said, "Give yourself some credit. You were only a freak for a few minutes."

She stared and curled her lips into that sarcastic smile she was so good at.

He grinned and said, "Now, you have my e-mail address, right?" She nodded. "And I have yours, so there's no reason we can't keep in touch."

"You got it!" she said with a single quick nod. "Have a good trip," she said as she turned toward the hotel.

"Thanks," he said. "You, too. Don't eat too much cheese!" They laughed as they parted and walked toward their respective hotels.

CHAPTER FOUR

It was 9:00 p.m. in The Netherlands and because it was so late, Chris checked in with no wait and no trouble.

"Here you are, Mr. Simonsez," the desk clerk smiled as she returned the credit card bearing the same name. I hope you'll find everything to your liking," she said cordially, handing him the room key.

"Thank you," he said, unable to conceal a grin at the name. He had pronounced it "See-MOAN-sez" for the desk clerk, although it was a take-off on his favorite childhood game, "Simon Says." He always used an assumed name when he traveled. That, coupled with a suitable disguise when he traveled outside America, normally prevented the sizeable crowds he usually drew in the States.

He opened the door to suite 1224 and dropped his portfolio on the mahogany drop leaf table in the foyer. He walked through the beautiful sitting room and into the lavish bedroom, plopping his backpack and suitcase on the bed, completely oblivious to his opulent surroundings. Luxury was the norm for Chris Lapp. He opened his suitcase, took out his laptop, connected it to the internet on the desk across the room then took Holly's e-mail address from his shirt pocket and quickly logged on. He clicked into his e-mail account and typed a short message to her. It read:

"You're not the only one who brought a laptop! I've added your e-mail address to my contacts list so you don't have to worry about me losing it now! Enjoy the t. and c.! Chris"

He pressed the "send" key then left the computer to unpack and relax in front of the TV. He channel surfed for awhile and found nothing to watch, at least nothing that he could understand. There seemed to be a program in every language except English. "Alas, I am unilingual!" he quoted from one of his movies as he laughed, turned off the TV and walked over to the large wing-back chair in the corner across from the computer. He sat down, removed his tennis shoes, leaned back against the blue-gray flowered chintz upholstery, and rested his feet on the matching footstool. His head fell against the tall back of the chair, and he started to think about the day's events. He couldn't understand how anyone could be afraid of flying. He did it so often, flying from one movie location to another to another and on to TV interviews, and from there to who-knows-where. It never crossed his mind to be afraid. Even more unbelievable was how quickly she had overcome the fear today. That was a mystery to him. She said she had prayed hard. He didn't understand that either.

Prayer was one of the most foreign things in the world to him. After all, it didn't help when his friend Arnold was sick. Arnold's parents had prayed for months, but he had died within six months of his benign brain tumor diagnosis. That was years ago, when he was nine years old, but he still remembered it clearly, even though he had only known Arnold that one year. He occasionally still missed Arnold from time to time, especially during baseball season. They had done everything together in that short time span, including play baseball on the same city team. Arnold was good...the best hitter on the team, probably in the whole city league. He wondered where Arnold was now.

"That woman has something," he said quietly. He was drawn to her but not as a man is usually drawn to a woman. It wasn't at all like that. It was...pure. He had never been drawn to anyone like that before. He couldn't understand the emotion, the feeling he was having. He wanted to know more about her, more about what she was thinking and how she was feeling. There had never been a character like her in any of his movies, male or female. He had nothing, no one, to relate to, to compare her to. He thought and wondered until his eyes became heavy and he drifted off to sleep.

Half an hour later he awoke to three musical notes coming from his computer. He stumbled over to the desk and saw that he had an e-mail...from Holly. He opened it and read:

"You never mentioned a laptop, you sneak! I plan to go to Lisse tomorrow and find those tulips. Guess I'll need to get up early for that. Maybe I'll happen upon a cheese shop on the way. Ha! Well, I've answered all my e-mails and am turning in. Enjoy your meetings. C ya. Holly"

He remembered that he hadn't actually told her he was attending meetings on this trip but instead had come here to get away for awhile, to be alone and think. Well, now he was thinking but it wasn't going nearly as he had anticipated. He was thinking about what she had said and about how upbeat she was, especially after she had "prayed hard" when she was so overcome with fear. What was that question she had asked him that had almost made him catch his breath? *If you died suddenly, do you know where you'd end up?* And she had asked him if he was happy with his life. If she only knew. In fact, it was as if she HAD known.

He had been so uneasy lately, so restless. He actually *had* begun thinking about where he'd be if he died. He had read script after script and book after book trying to come up with a project that would distract him from the dissatisfaction of his present life. His latest movie had just wrapped, and he was coming here to get away for some much-needed rest but instead he was more restless than ever. And confused.

He called room service and ordered a bottle of his favorite wine. It came shortly and he opened it and poured a large glassful. He took a couple of swallows and pushed it aside. Why wasn't it as satisfying as he usually found it? He took out a cigarette and lit it. After three or four puffs, he extinguished it in the ashtray on his bedside table. It was like there was a hole in his soul that nothing could fill. The only thing he could think of to alleviate his misery was to go to bed and try to sleep...at least he wouldn't be thinking then. Maybe he should go down to the bar and see if there was someone there who might be suitable "company" for the night. Oddly enough, he wasn't interested.

Back at The Crimson Tulip there had been no trouble with Holly's check-in either. She had turned down the bellman's offer to escort her to her room and instead had asked if there was somewhere she could buy a snack. The gift shop was still open and they had crackers and soft drinks. She made her purchase, found the elevators and went up to her room. As she put the key in the door, she said to herself, *Well, room 377, for the next three nights it's just you and me.*

She found the room nicer than she had expected, with a large picture window facing the canal in the back and, yes, there was a vase of tulips but not just yellow ones...yellow ones and red ones, their favorite colors. *You are a dear,* she thought of her husband as she smiled and touched them tenderly. She placed her purse next to them on the coffee table and opened the card. "To my brave darling," it read. Tears welled up in her eyes as she reached for her cell phone and pressed the "home" speed dial key.

In a moment he answered, "Hello?"

"Hey, Baby," she choked through the tears.

"Are you all right?" he asked with concern in his voice.

"I'm fine...very, very fine," she answered.

"How was the flight?" he asked anxiously.

"It went unusually well. I freaked a little at first, but," she hesitated then said, "I asked Jesus for help, and He came through, as usual." She changed the subject. "The tulips are gorgeous. Thank you so much. You didn't have to do that."

"I know I didn't, but I knew you deserved them," he answered. "And what if I had not done well?" she asked.

He quickly said, "Then you would have NEEDED them." They laughed and she told him about the trip and how it had started off so badly and ended up so well. For some reason she decided not to tell him whom God had used to help her through the ordeal in the beginning. That would be a longer story than she was willing to devote the time to right now, but she did tell him how God had answered her cry to Him when she had called on the name of Jesus. She wanted God to have all the glory for that.

They talked awhile longer and, after she had caught up on their shopping spree and trip back to Wells, they said their goodbyes, and she prepared for bed.

The sheets were cool as she lay in the big king-size bed thinking about her marvelous day and contemplating the next two. She thanked God for all the blessings of that day and asked Him to guide her steps on the remainder of this trip, asking Him not to let her miss any opportunities that He wanted her to take advantage of to speak to someone about Him. She prayed for protection for her family and herself. She also prayed for Chris to be drawn to Jesus.

"Father, Jesus says in John 6:44, 'No one can come to Me unless the Father Who sent Me draws him, and I will raise him up at the last day.' Well, Father, I'm asking you now to draw Chris to you. Thank You, Lord. In Jesus' Name, Amen." She yawned, turned over and drifted into a peaceful sleep.

At the Adell, Chris stirred, woke up and looked at the clock. "Oh-h-h-h," he groaned, "12:30?" He fell back on his pillow and eventually drifted back to sleep. Two hours later, he stirred, awoke and checked the time again. "What?" he was barely able to think aloud. "Only 2:35?" Sleep came in two- and three-hour intervals until around 7:00 a.m. when he finally chose getting up over fighting for sleep. He stumbled to the window, parted the cream-colored curtains slightly and looked out onto a city just awakening to the new day. Under a gray dawn sky he could barely detect the headlights of a bus passing by on the street underneath his window, then a police car slowly patrolling the area, several cars and then a street sweeper making the streets ready for another busy day. A few *bakfiets* riders maneuvering their boxed-in two-wheelers silently ended the snaking line of vehicles.

Chris turned and headed for the bathroom. After his shower, he dressed and sat down in the wing-back chair again. *I came here to rest,* he thought. *So why can't I?* He sat with his head cradled against the high back of the chair again, wondering what was wrong with him. Then he thought of Holly and the strange feeling she gave him. He finally faced the fact that nothing would do except to talk with her again, hoping that something would be gained from the conversation that would alleviate his restlessness.

Realizing he shouldn't call her at 7:30 in the morning, he wondered how he could arrange a time to talk with her, and he didn't think he could wait long. Remembering that she had said she would get up early to go to Lisse to see the tulips, he decided he would go to The Crimson Tulip and wait for her outside.

He grabbed his denim jacket, stuffed his wallet, fat money clip and room key into his jeans pocket and headed downstairs. Getting off the elevator he noticed the coffee shop he had ignored last night, went in and purchased a blueberry muffin and a cup of black coffee to go. He walked down the block to The Crimson Tulip and stationed himself on a bench at the end of the walkway leading to the front doors to watch for her to come out. Half an hour passed and he didn't see any sign of her.

Women, he thought almost grumpily. *Why does it take so long for them to get ready to go anywhere?* He shook his head and thought, *Well, I'll just wait her out.*

Inside room 377 she had actually been ready to go for awhile but, as always, sat down for a time of Bible reading, prayer and listening for God to speak. Sometimes He spoke and sometimes He didn't. She didn't seem to hear Him speak this morning, but she had a feeling that God was preparing her for a divine appointment, an opportunity to talk with someone about Him. She hoped so and picked up her purse and camera, heading out the door for the elevator in anticipation.

She got off the elevator and, remembering the small airy café in the lobby, she walked up and sat down at the nearest table. The server, Marie, came over immediately, handed her a menu and asked if she wanted coffee. "No, but I would like pineapple juice, if you have it," she answered with a questioning look.

"Surely," came the cordial reply. In a moment, Marie came back with the juice and asked for her order. Grateful that the menu had English translations, Holly had made her selection and was ready.

"A Belgian waffle, thank you," was her response.

"Thank you," the tall, pretty brunette said with a shy smile and a slight bow.

Outside Chris was wondering if he had missed Holly, if maybe she had left earlier than he had assumed. *Surely she didn't leave before dawn!* he wondered. After a few minutes, he decided to go inside the hotel in hopes of meeting her in the lobby. He walked through one of the three revolving doors, through the foyer and into the lobby where he immediately spotted her in the café reading the book she had brought along.

He walked up beside her and said, "You know you're not going to get that book read on this trip, don't you?"

She looked up from her book, eyes widening as she said, "What a surprise!"

He smiled and said, "May I join you?"

She said, "Of course!" Then, "I would think you'd be preparing for your meeting."

He raised his eyebrows, cocked his head to one side and said, "I never told you I was here for a meeting."

She thought for a second then said, "No, you didn't, did you? You just said you travel a lot on business. So what brings you here this time?"

He looked down for a moment then looked everywhere except her eyes and said, "Just needed to get away for awhile for a little 'R&R.'"

She knew better than to ask anything more about it and changed the subject. "So what're you planning to do today, 'R' or 'R?'"

He chuckled and said slowly, "Wel-l-l, actually I was wondering if you had your heart set on seeing those tulips alone?" She shrugged and said, "Not at all. In fact, I was sorta wondering if I was going to get a little tired of myself, if you want to know the truth."

He nodded then asked sheepishly, "Would you mind if I tag along?"

She shook her head, smiled and said, "I'd probably enjoy the company." *Probably? How's that for an understatement?*

Just then Marie brought the waffle and syrup and asked if Chris would like anything. "Just coffee, black, thank you... uh...in a to-go cup, please" he replied with a smile, noticing that Holly's plate was almost empty. She looked at him a moment then bowed slightly and walked away. In a moment she returned with the cup and set it in front of him.

She started to walk away then turned back, blue eyes squinting, and asked, "Do I know you?"

Uh-oh, Holly thought, and cut another piece of waffle, looking away as she chewed.

"No, I don't think so," he responded and looked down at his cup, hoping the bill of his cap would deter her scrutiny.

"Oh, I'm sorry," she apologized.

"No problem," he smiled.

Holly knew Marie would probably go back and tell the other servers that she suspected she was serving Chris Lapp, so she said, "Well, I think I've had enough. You ready?" Then she motioned for Marie and asked her for the check.

Chris quickly said, "Put hers on mine." Marie performed her customary bow and quickly walked away.

She looked at Chris in awe and said, "Am I going to pay for any of my meals on this trip?"

He pretended not to smile and said, "Probably not."

She grinned and said, "Thank you very much."

"Not at all," was his reply. Marie was back soon with the check and Chris handed her a bill and said, "Keep the change."

She looked at the bill and gave him a very wide smile and purred, "Thank you *very* much," and walked away folding the bill and tucking it safely into her pocket.

"Apparently someone is a very generous tipper," Holly said to him as they both rose from their seats.

"I was a waiter back in the day," he said. "Payback." She gave him an understanding nod, picked up her purse and camera and they started out the door. Coming through the revolving door and outside for the first time that day, she was glad she had worn jeans and a light jacket. It held off the slight chill in the air. The short sleeved t-shirt underneath would be enough in the afternoon sun later on.

CHAPTER FIVE

As they started down the walkway to the street, Chris stopped abruptly and said, "You know what we forgot?" Holly stopped and thought for a few seconds, with furrowed brow.

"I can't think of a thing. What are you talking about?"

"The picture."

"What picture?"

"We were going to find someone at the airport to take our pictures with our cameras, and we forgot all about it!"

"Yes we did!" she remembered. "I bet we can find someone who'll do that for us," she said as she looked first to the right and then to the left, searching for a pedestrian who might accommodate them.

"I left mine in my room," he said.

"That's okay. We'll use mine and I'll scan it to you when I get home."

"Okay," he agreed, but she could hear the disappointment in his voice.

"Ah, here comes a nice-looking gentleman now. I bet he'll do it," she said confidently.

"Excuse me, sir," Chris said to the grandfatherly looking man. "Would you take our picture?"

He nodded and smiled, taking her camera. "No English," he said as he shrugged apologetically and put the camera to his eye. They backed up a few feet, posed, and smiled. The language barrier made it useless to attempt a more picturesque shot, so they just let him snap a couple and thanked him as best they could by shaking his hand as he handed the camera back to her and went on his way.

"You'll want to take some more pictures today, so why don't you go get your camera, and I'll wait here on this bench, okay?" she asked him, taking a seat on the same bench where he had waited for her earlier.

"Okay, be back in a minute," he said as he strode toward the Adell. She watched his steps turn into a trot as he went the twenty-five yards or so back to his hotel. In a few minutes she saw him come through the revolving door and trot back to the bench where he found her looking over a brochure about a shuttle service that would take them to Lisse and back. It would be along in about ten minutes and pick them up right where they were.

"If it starts to rain, we'll be in trouble. Why don't you let me rent a car?" he offered. "That way, we'll be on your schedule, not the shuttle's."

She considered it, then shrugged and said, "It's your dime. That'd be great."

They went into The Crimson Tulip and asked the concierge about rental cars. She gave them information about a company that would deliver the car to the hotel within 30 minutes. "Great!" he enthused. "Well, you want to just sit here and wait for it?" he asked, looking around the lobby.

Holly agreed, and they found a seat with a clear shot of the doors and waited for the car's arrival.

As they waited they began talking about yesterday's flight. He was curious as to what had given her such a fear of flying. She explained about her first flight as a 17-year-old high school senior and how well that had gone and then about flying eight years later and how well that had gone then a couple of years later when the fear had come after the two bumpy flights to Washington, D.C. and back.

"I don't understand it myself," she explained, "but I think it has something to do with waiting so long between flights. I was so young and naive and unafraid at 17...and so excited to finally be going somewhere. I love to travel, so the fear has really hampered my life." She was silent a moment, then added, "And my husband's." She looked down, thinking about all she had robbed him of because of her silly fears. A tear came into her eye, and she looked away, hoping Chris wouldn't see it. She had cried enough yesterday, she thought. He was unwrapping a piece of gum and walking over to a trash can to dispose of the paper. She took the opportunity to wipe away the tear.

He took his seat again. "I'm trying to quit smoking," he said, making a disgusted face. "Want some?" He offered her the pack.

She accepted a stick gratefully. "I don't smoke, but I do chew," she said, laughing at her own joke. She stuck her nose in the air and in her best Scarlett O'Hara voice gushed, "I don't smoke, and I don't chew, and I don't run with them that do."

He laughed out loud and asked, "Where in the world did you learn that?"

"Don't tell me you've never heard that little piece of Southern poetry!" she exclaimed.

"Never!" he said bending over, still laughing. "Can I use that?"

She laughed and said as she unwrapped the piece of gum, "You don't get out much, do ya? Sure, use it..I stole it from someone myself."

They both quieted and glanced toward the door, just in case the car was early. Turning back to her he asked, "So you think you've robbed your husband of one of life's little pleasures...flying?" Oh, dear. He was returning to the issue she thought she had so eloquently evaded.

"Well," she began, "of course, he says I haven't robbed him of anything, but it surely seems like it to me. We both like to travel and since the Washington flights, it's been necessary to travel by car or train, and when it's by car, he does all the driving, even though I offer to help." She stopped and looked back toward the door. "He says I don't drive fast enough for him," she added, making a sarcastic face. "He says driving is relaxing to him. Now, I gotta tell ya, driving does not relax me...it does the opposite...tenses me up."

He gave a slight grin then said, "I gotta agree with him. It relaxes me, too. I like to drive. It's a good time for thinking."

Just then a tall thin man in a crisp uniform strode through the door and into the lobby. "Ah, that must be our man," Chris said rising from his chair.

"I'll stay with our things," she told him. Chris nodded his acknowledgment then strode to meet the man. They completed the transaction, the man handed Chris the key to the car, Chris handed him a generous tip, then the man smiled, tipped his hat to them both and left with a co-worker who was waiting for him in another car.

Chris returned to her and picked up his camera. "Ready?"

She gathered her things and answered, "Sure thing. Let's boogie." They went out to the waiting car, put their things in the back seat, and left for Lisse. "Do we know where we're going?" she asked as they pulled into traffic.

"Sorta," he answered with a fair amount of confidence. "I think if we follow these signs we'll come to a directional overhead sign," he said as he motioned to a couple of signs along the block on the left. They had three red tulips and an arrow that pointed straight ahead.

They found their way out of town soon enough, passing beautiful old red brick buildings, canals, and vendors selling brightly colored flowers of all kinds, and were able to gain highway speed. They were silent for several miles when she said, "Relaxing or thinking?"

He seemed to return from far away and said, "Huh?... Oh, a little of both." She waited for him to elaborate, but he didn't, so she let it lay...for the moment. *Give him a little more time,* she thought. She was desperately hoping he was mulling over their conversation on the plane. *Hmmm,* she thought, suddenly remembering this morning's suspicion of a divine appointment.

They rode on another ten or fifteen minutes in silence, then he asked, "Remember asking me on the plane yesterday about whether I'm happy with my life?"

"Yeah," she answered, hiding the anticipation she was feeling.

"Well, the answer is 'no,' and I really can't figure out why," he admitted.

She thought a moment then asked, "Could it have anything to do with the answer to the other question I asked you at that same time?"

He thought a bit then looked at her and said, "You mean the one about where I'd go if I suddenly died?" She nodded. "Could those two be related?" he wondered aloud.

"They definitely are," she affirmed. Silence. She gave him time to think.

A long while later he said, "I can't go there right now."

She said, "Okay. No problem." Then she said to God, *You love him, Lord. If You want me to pursue this, please tell me how. Have him question me or something so I'll know how to talk to him. You know, I don't live in his world, so it's hard for me to relate to him.*

God seemed to say to her, *He's just a human being like anyone else. Relate to him on human terms.* She resolved to do just that but waited for him to open the door again. She knew it might be hours, so she settled herself in and determined to just enjoy the day and wait for an opportune time to speak.

Soon they entered the town of Lisse and slowed down to look for signs that might point the way to the areas where the tulips were in bloom. They began to notice signs like the one they had seen in Amsterdam with the three red tulips and an arrow that pointed in the direction they should turn.

In no time they were outside the city itself and riding in the country again. About two miles from town they topped a hill and she gasped. "Oh!" was all she could manage to say. The tears streamed down her cheeks as she stared first out his window then out hers. There were tulips on both sides of the road as far as the eye could see, red on the left side and yellow on the right. He was taken aback at her emotion and soon found a place to pull the car over. He sat very still, allowing her to absorb it all. She was embarrassed and, looking down, said quietly, "I just never thought I'd see them, that's all."

He said, "It's all right. Take your time and enjoy it."

She smiled and reached into the back seat for her purse. When she had retrieved it, she took out a tissue and remembered the last time she had done that. It was on the plane, and she was crying from fear. This time it was from pure joy. She had conquered her fear of flying and was actually experiencing a sight she had dreamed of for more than forty years. *Yet in all these things we are more than conquerors through Him Who loved us.* That verse always gave her strength.

He noticed up ahead a sign that pointed to an entrance and realized that this was actually a public gardens area, so he steered the car back onto the road and drove the hundred yards or so to the gate. He stopped at the fee stand and paid the fee to enter then drove the car in and found a parking spot. They got out of the car, cameras in tow, and walked along a path that wound through some of the closest rows of flowers.

There was a paved trail that snaked all through the park, and around every curve she marveled at the different colors and varieties of tulips. Besides the red and yellow, there were pink, white, orange, purple and even one variety that was almost black. There were Darwins and Parrots and many others. She was overwhelmed and took so many pictures that she wondered what she would do with all of them. *God, You are good,* she whispered once as she looked across the fields. She didn't realize that Chris had heard her and watched her in amazement. This was a place of joy for her, a dream come true, and he didn't want to do anything to disturb her bliss.

He saw a bench under some trees, quietly slipped over to it, and sat down. He watched her walk by the rows and bend and gently touch every variety within reach. Using his zoom lens once, he snapped a couple of shots of her when her joy-filled face was in view. She didn't even realize he had slipped away, and he sat in awe of how this could possibly make her so happy. He had seen so much of the world and realized now, for the first time, that he was taking everything in his life for granted. What if he did indeed die suddenly and had never stopped, as she had, to smell the roses? He smiled slightly at the little pun then stared off into space, contemplating the shallowness of his life.

He didn't even notice her walking toward him until he heard her say, "There you are. Did you get tired? We can go if you want to."

"No! No! I was just sitting and thinking," he assured her.

"Anything in particular?" she asked, hopeful.

"Nah, just thinking," he answered with a wave of his hand. "My muffin and coffee are gone. You hungry?" he asked, quickly changing the subject.

"As a matter of fact, I was just going to suggest lunch," she said, slinging her camera and purse over her shoulder.

"Good," he said. "I see a sidewalk café down that way," he said, pointing down the paved path and to his right. They walked toward it in silence. There was no line, so they stepped up, quickly looked over the menu, ordered sandwiches and soft drinks and took a seat at one of the little glass-topped black wrought-iron tables. It was covered with a soft yellow tablecloth embossed with the familiar logo, three red tulips. He took a bite of his sandwich and a swallow of his drink then got up and walked back to the window. He came back with a napkin and laid it in front of her. It had something rolled up in it.

"What's this?" she asked curiously.

"Open it," he said. She looked at him cautiously. "It won't bite," he laughed. She picked it up and carefully unwrapped it. Into her hand fell a small piece of yellow cheese. She gave him a confused look.

"I didn't hear me ask for cheese," she quipped laying it back on the napkin and placing the napkin on the table between them.

"You didn't," he said, but I figure it's a preview of your next mission." She laughed as she got the joke.

"Cheese shopping?"

"Cheese shopping," he repeated.

She laughed again and said, "You crack me up!"

They finished their meal and sat for a minute enjoying the sun. They had expected the typical cloudy skies of The Netherlands, but the weather was perfect, so nice, in fact, that they doffed their jackets and hung them on the rounded backs of their chairs, which were imprinted with the tulip logo.

"Want to share the mission preview?" she asked, unwrapping the cheese again and cutting it in two.

"Sure," he said, reaching for his half.

She bit off a piece and chewed for a few seconds. "Nice," she commented, nodding her head in approval. "What kind is it?"

"Gouda," he said.

She laughed and said, "I've always liked that word, 'Gouda.'" Sounds like a Scandinavian name, you know, like, Olga, Helga...Gouda."

"Ha! You're right. I never thought of it that way," he laughed.

They finished the cheese then she said, "I think there's one more area around the curve in the pathway with more tulips, and I'd like to get a look at them before we leave. Okay with you?"

"Sure. Wouldn't want to miss anything," he said.

"Great. You ready?" she asked, gathering up her paper products and rising to throw them away.

"Yeah, let's hit the dusty trail," he said as he rose with his trash, not realizing he had quoted a line from his only western. Holly grinned. They threw the trash away in the nearby receptacle then got their jackets and other belongings and walked the fifty or so feet to the last flower beds. These were not fields but large beds of all colors and varieties of tulips. The beds were built on an incline and in the distance where the tulips met the sky stood an alabaster windmill, tall and straight, as if guarding a treasure.

"Just breathtaking!" she exclaimed as she took the lens cap off her camera and readied it for the last couple of shots.

"Here," he said, laying his things down on a nearby bench. "You stand in front of them, and I'll snap you." She walked over and stood in front of the largest bed and he snapped the picture.

Just then a young girl walked up to him and said, "Excuse me. Would you like to stand with her? I'll take one for you."

"Oh, thank you," he said handing her the camera. He pointed to her and yelled over to Holly, smiling, "An American!" He showed her the button to press then walked over and positioned himself beside Holly.

"Can you get the windmill in the background?" Holly asked, pointing behind her.

"Sure can," the pretty blonde answered, eye to the viewfinder. "Say 'Dutch cheese!'"

"How appropriate!" Chris snickered. Holly giggled. The young American tourist snapped a couple of shots then walked over and handed him the camera. They thanked her and she waved as she walked away, blue eyes smiling.

She looked over her shoulder as she left them and said, "Now you do something nice for someone else." They smiled and nodded as they waved after her.

"That was really nice of her," Holly said as they went back to the bench to get his things. They strolled back through the gardens to the rented car, got in and, as they drove out the exit, she sighed and said, "That was one of the most awesome sights I've ever seen. It's amazing to me that God created such complex beings as us, scoundrels that we are sometimes, and also such delicate, innocent things as tulips." She paused a couple of seconds then added, "And the reason He created such delicate things as tulips was to please such complex beings as us." She shook her head. "Simply amazing."

"Yeah," was all the response he could manage. The amazing thing to him right now was that she squeezed every drop out of life and seemed to enjoy the simplest things. Things that most people take for granted...or don't pay any attention to at all. How did she manage to do that?

They were quiet until they entered Lisse again, and when he turned right and parked in front of a group of shops, she asked, "What're we doing?" He leaned down so that he could point through the windshield to one of the shops.

"Your next mission."

She leaned down and saw a photography studio, a sandwich shop, a florist...and a cheese shop. A wide smile appeared on her face. "Cheese shopping?" she inquired, eyebrows raised.

"Cheese shopping," he confirmed. They laughed, got out of the car and headed for the shop. As they pushed the door open, a little bell rang in the doorway over their heads. The atmosphere was a mixture of aromas: sweet cheddar, tangy Swiss, pungent Limberger, and lots of others. She chose several and asked that they be shipped to her home in the States. The clerk was fluent in English and very accommodating.

When she gave the total to Holly, Chris presented his credit card. "No," she said quietly to him. "I can't let you continue to pay for my trip." He looked at her with surprise.

"Please," he said, equally quiet. "It's just something I want to do, okay?" There was something in his eyes. Pain? Was there something comforting to him about paying for her things all day? She looked at the clerk and nodded her head then looked back at him. He smiled with relief and handed the clerk his card. She completed the transaction, he signed the ticket, and they went back to the car, bell ringing as the door closed behind them.

They were quiet for a couple of miles, then she said, "Thank you so much for all you've done for me today. You shouldn't have, but I appreciate it very much. Please don't think I've taken it all for granted."

A look of surprise came over his face as he peered at her and said, "You're kidding, right?"

She shook her head and said, "No," with her own look of surprise.

"I don't think you could take anything for granted if you tried!" he exclaimed.

"Why on earth would you say such a thing?" she cried.

"Because," he said, calming down. "You just seem so genuine...so appreciative...so unassuming...so...real." He said the last word as if he'd found the word he was looking for.

She laughed as she said, "Well, thank you." He didn't say anything else. They rode on for a few more miles, then she said, "I was right about the vase of tulips."

He looked puzzled. "Vase of tulips?"

She said, "The vase of tulips I predicted would be in my room when I checked in."

He remembered and said, "He sent them, then?" She nodded and smiled.

"Yeah, and not just yellow ones like I thought but yellow ones and red ones, our favorite colors. When our daughter was born he sent me yellow and red silk roses. I still have them." She was quiet then said, "That man is something else."

He nodded slowly and said, "You deserve a 'something else' kind of man."

It embarrassed her a little so Holly did what she always did when she wanted to wiggle out of a situation...she cracked a joke. Putting on her best Scarlett O'Hara again, she said, "Why, Mr. Simonsez, how you do talk!" She had pronounced it "Simon Says," but he knew what she was referring to. His mouth dropped open and he couldn't think of a thing to say at first. She let out a hearty laugh at his reaction.

When he regained his wits, he repeated, "Mr. Simonsez?"

She laughed and said, "Yeah, I saw it on your credit card. Quite by accident," she quickly added.

He got a little nervous, fearing the inevitable third degree. He really still believed Holly didn't know who he was and that if she discovered his true identity, she would be just another star-struck groveler.

"Relax," she said with a smile. "It's okay." Somehow he knew it was and the subject was dropped.

They grew quiet again. Tulips and cheese. It seemed to take so little to make her happy...or maybe everything made her happy. He still didn't know what it was about her that drew him, but it had to do with her attitude, he thought. After awhile he became solemn as it occurred to him: *Could it have to do with her God?*

He was deep in thought when she yawned and said, "I've never had jet lag before, but I'm thinking this is it."

He said, "I've had it before and you're looking it."

She made a face. "Thanks a lot!"

"Sorry, but you know what I mean. You probably didn't see it coming and now you're forced to be still and quiet. And riding in a car on top of that. That monotonous droning will put you out like a baby. It'll just creep up on you," he said with a warning tone in his voice. She propped her arm on the door and leaned on it.

"I guess I'd better call it a day, then. I want to be fresh for tomorrow."

He raised his eyebrows and asked, "Oh, yeah? What's your plan for tomorrow?"

She shrugged and said, "I don't have a clue. I did the tulips and cheese thing all in one day, so I guess I need to make a new plan tonight. Maybe something will come to me. Then I'll probably call home, check my e-mails, have a room service supper and turn in." She looked over at him and asked, "What about you? What's your plan for tomorrow, R or R?"

He laughed and said, "Well, like you, I don't have a plan yet either, but it'll either be R or R!" But to himself he was thinking there wouldn't be any rest OR relaxation...not with such a confused mind. Today he was busy and had someone to help occupy his mind. Tomorrow wasn't looking as promising. He might actually be forced to think about the restlessness in his troubled soul.

In a short while, they pulled up in front of The Crimson Tulip, left the car there, and went inside where he left the key with the desk clerk as he had been instructed. The clerk would call the rental company and someone would pick up the car as soon as possible.

He turned to her and said, "I had a really great time today. Thanks for letting me tag along. I don't know what I would have done otherwise." He scratched the back of his head, one hand on his hip.

She smiled and said, "It's I that should be thanking you. You just took care of everything all day." He went bashful again, smiled and looked down at the floor. She almost expected him to say, "Aw, shucks."

Instead he looked up and said, "If you find yourself with nothing to do tomorrow, give me a call. We'll go sightseeing or something."

She considered it and said, "Since I'll probably sleep in, why don't you give me a call after lunch?"

His face brightened as he said, "Are you sure? You're not getting tired of me?"

"Heck, no!" was her only response. She would rather have screamed, "Getting tired of Chris Lapp? Are you mad?"

He picked up his camera from the desk and said, "Okay, then. I'll call you around 1:00."

She smiled and said, "Okay, I'll be waiting." They waved as he walked out the door and she went to the elevator.

CHAPTER SIX

Holly's evening was short and just as she predicted: she called home, checked her e-mails, ate and went to bed, falling asleep immediately and sleeping through the night, something she hadn't done in a long time.

Chris, on the other hand, had another rough evening. After having a room service meal, channel surfing for awhile, looking out his window and thinking, he still couldn't sleep. He remembered his wine, went into the kitchen and retrieved it from the refrigerator. He always liked it really cold. It was room temperature last time...maybe that's why it didn't satisfy him. He poured a small glass, took a few swallows, then poured it and the rest of the bottle down the sink. It was like drinking water, except now it tasted bad. He paced through the bright, white kitchen with its golden and sea foam accents, the beautifully appointed dining area, the elaborate sitting room and into the massive bedroom. Then he repeated the trek, unable to appreciate the beauty and comfort around him and all the time wondering what was happening to him. He passed by the pack of cigarettes on the night stand, stood a moment, then picked it up and tried to smoke one. He soon crushed it out in the ashtray. There was just nothing to it any more. He plodded to the bathroom and threw the pack in the trash can.

He walked into the sitting room and, realizing he had spent no time in there, plopped down on the elegant blue-gray sofa and turned on the television. One of his movies was airing. "Ugh! No way am I sitting through that," he grimaced, then noticed that it was dubbed and watched for a few minutes, slightly amused at how awkward it was to watch the lips and sound operate out of sync. It relaxed him enough so that he thought he could fall asleep, and he yawned and ambled to the bathroom to brush his teeth.

As he squeezed toothpaste onto his toothbrush, he looked in the mirror. "Boy, you look rough." He felt rough, too. And lonely. Tomorrow was going to be difficult. He had planned to stay a week, but maybe he would just go home. Staying here alone would only prove to heighten his misery. He slid between the clean white sheets of the big king-sized bed and fell asleep immediately, exhausted from his own case of jet lag and emotional misery. Quite unexpectedly, he slept soundly all night.

At 10:00 the next morning he awakened feeling surprisingly refreshed and looked at the clock on his night stand in disbelief. *I slept till ten? I can't believe I slept at all!* he thought in amazement. He yawned and stretched and sat up in the middle of the bed looking out the window. He had been so upset and tired when he went to bed that he forgot to close the curtains, but he was glad now to soak in the sun that was streaming in. However, even though he was well rested physically, he knew the rest of him was still in trouble, so he sat there for awhile pondering whether to leave or stay. In three hours he was supposed to call Holly to see what she wanted to do. He didn't even know if he'd still be in Amsterdam then.

He was hungry, so he showered, dressed, grabbed his wallet, money clip, and room key and went downstairs to the restaurant, glad to discover that breakfast was still being served. Thankfully, the restaurant wasn't busy at all, and no one recognized him. The sunglasses and hat continued to prove a suitable disguise. After a hearty breakfast, he just sat there pondering. He really needed company to take his mind off whatever was going on inside him, so he decided to stay and call Holly at 1:00. It was 11:00 now, so he decided to go back to his suite, get his jacket and take a walk to kill some time...and think.

He stepped outside and found the sky still sunny, even though the weather report on TV last night had suggested clouds and a shower or two. Okay, so the sunglasses would actually make sense today.

He had been walking for about half an hour or so when he realized he was coming up on The Crimson Tulip for the third time. He looked at his watch and saw that it was approaching noon. *I wonder...* he thought as he stopped at the bench where he had waited for Holly yesterday morning. He strode up the walkway and through one of the revolving doors. Yep, there she was at the same table, having lunch and reading her book. "You know you're not going to get that book read on this trip, don't you?" he asked as he put his hand on the chair across from her.

"A gentleman asked me that very question yesterday!" she said as she smiled and invited him to sit down. "Would you like to order something?" she asked.

"No, no. Actually, I just ate breakfast," he answered, leaning his elbows on the table and resting his chin on his hands.

"What?! Breakfast? How long have you been awake?" she asked in amazement.

"You wouldn't believe how well I slept," he answered. "I didn't wake up until ten."

"Wow, me, too," she said. "Well, 9:45," she corrected as she put her book away.

He said, "I finished eating around 11:00, so I decided to take a walk and ended up here. Hope you don't mind."

"'Course not," she assured him. "So what's the plan for today?" she asked, wiping her mouth and laying her napkin on the table to get her purse. As she got out her wallet, he reached for the check. She squinted at him, picked up a knife and said, "Touch it and draw back a nub."

He was caught completely off guard and laughed uncontrollably. When he could breathe again he asked, "Where do you get these sayings?"

She grinned and put the knife down. "I have my sources."

She put her credit card on the check as Claude, the server, was approaching the table. Claude whisked it away with a smile and a quick "I'll be back in a moment."

Holly turned her attention back to Chris and said, "Okay, back to the question...what's the plan for today?"

"I don't know," he answered shrugging. "What about you?"

"Well," she began. "I want to buy some souvenirs for my family, but I don't want to get them here at the hotel. Didn't we pass a little gift shop on the way to Lisse yesterday?"

He thought a minute and said, "Yeah, actually it was only about three blocks from here."

"Yeah," she remembered, "on the right. I think it was called Van Cleef's. Let's go there."

"Okay. You up for a three-block walk?" he asked as Claude returned with her credit card.

"Sure," she said as she signed the receipt. They rose from the table and went out into the sunny courtyard in front.

"Don't tell me," she said, holding up one hand. "You left your camera again."

"Yeah, but I don't think I'll need it this time," he came back.

"Okay. Well, let's go then," she said walking off with a spring in her step. It was really nice outside and they enjoyed the walk, talking about the buildings and the various window displays as they passed quaint little shops and a couple of larger department stores.

In no time they were at Van Cleef's and they entered the heavy old door. There was no tinkling bell this time, but one electronic "ding" as they passed a censor in the doorway. There were all kinds of souvenirs that one might expect to see in The Netherlands: a variety of items with a tulip motif, cheese boards with little serrated knives and pretty glass covers, wooden shoes, wind chimes, bird houses and feeders, miniature windmills, and a vast array of what Holly deemed "souvenirish-looking" items. She chose gifts for each family member and several friends then asked if the clerk could wrap them in heavy paper for packing in her suitcase, which she gladly did. Chris even bought himself a snow globe with a yellow tulip in it.

"I bet every time I look at this I'll remember fields of tulips and eating cheese at Lisse," he said with a laugh. They completed their transactions and headed back out onto the sidewalk.

"Where to now?" she asked adjusting her purse on her shoulder and getting a better grip on her shopping bag, grateful she had chosen small gifts. She didn't notice he was turning the snow globe over and over in his hands and staring at it as he stood still waiting for her. She started to walk and noticed that he didn't move. "You okay?" she asked bending a little to look at his face. He always wore those blasted sunglasses and she could never really see his eyes. In fact, she hadn't seen his eyes on the whole trip, but she knew the reason and hadn't mentioned it.

"No," he said quietly. "Do you think we could go somewhere quiet and just talk?"

"Absolutely," she answered. "I really didn't have anything else planned and I think I'd enjoy just sitting and talking. Got any place in mind?" They looked up and down the street, and he remembered a park a block or two into town and suggested they go there. He thought he remembered lots of benches under some trees, so they walked the two blocks further and found a comfortable place in the shade away from pedestrian traffic. It was a nice big park bench with room to put their things between them, so they made themselves at home.

"This is going to be a serious talk, isn't it?" she asked quietly. He was leaned over, forearms on his legs, hands clasped between his knees, looking down.

"Yeah," he said without moving.

"Then you're going to have to take off your sunglasses," she said. He looked up, surprised.

"Huh?" he asked. She pointed to his face.

"Your sunglasses. When I talk seriously with people, I like to see their eyes. Call me weird." He looked around as he reached for the glasses. No one was in sight, so he slowly removed them and looked up at her in anticipation. "You don't have to hide behind them anymore. I know who you are," she said kindly. His eyes grew wide and his lips parted slightly.

"What?" he asked in disbelief.

"I've known ever since you boarded the plane," she said with a smile. "You're Chris Lapp." He didn't know what to say. She was quiet and let him think for a moment.

When he could speak again, he asked, "Why haven't you said something?"

Her smile grew wider as she said, "Well, I figured that everyone is always hanging on to you, wanting something, fawning all over you. I would think that you would get pretty tired of that, and I didn't want to do that to you. I have too much respect for you. Besides, you're my favorite."

"Favorite?"

"I know you've heard it a thousand times before, so here comes the old cliche. You're my favorite actor." He smiled and looked down. She added, "So why would I want to add to your trouble? If you like someone and respect them, you don't do that." His face relaxed and he looked relieved.

He stared at her for a minute, then he said, "I'm truly amazed. This is the first time I have ever encountered anything like this. I don't know what to say."

"Say, 'Thank you, Holly,'" she teased.

"Thank you, Holly," he mimicked. He looked a little embarrassed then said, "This trip has actually been very refreshing. I haven't felt like I've had to hide from people all the time."

She laughed and said, "Well, I have to admit it," she said, pointing to his constant companions. "It's been a very convincing disguise...the sunglasses, the hat."

He laughed and said, "Yeah, it works pretty well...most of the time."

Then she said matter-of-factly, "But you can't hide those cheekbones, sonny. I'm surprised more people haven't recognized you. That's the first thing I noticed when you got on the plane."

"Really? No kidding?" he queried.

"No kidding."

"Hmmm," he said, rubbing his chin. "Guess next time I'll have to glue on a beard or something." Holly giggled.

They were quiet, then she said, "Now...what were we going to talk so seriously about?"

"Oh, yeah," he said, looking thoughtful again. "Well, to tell you the truth, I've been pretty miserable lately and I'm not sure why."

A look of concern came over her face as she asked, "Miserable? Like unhappy?"

He nodded and leaned back against the bench and said, "Yeah, unhappy, restless, like nothing I do satisfies me. I come here to try and get away, I smoke, I drink my favorite wine which usually brings me comfort..."

"Or maybe numbs the *dis*comfort?" she interrupted.

"Well, I'm beginning to wonder," he said. "I read books and scripts searching for something to make me feel alive, but nothing seems to draw me. Nothing is interesting anymore. I feel like there's a hole in my soul."

Bang! Just what she had been listening for. She knew that what he was describing was his need for the Lord but was waiting for the opportunity to broach the subject with him again. "Can I tell you something? I mean, can I be perfectly honest with you?" she asked him.

"Well, sure."

"I've been exactly where you are. I mean, not walked in those same shoes but I've been in a desert place. It was dry and I felt unfulfilled and couldn't make sense of it. Nothing I tried would fill the void because..." she hesitated, silently asking God to help her say what He wanted her to say and to prepare Chris to hear it. "...to tell you the absolute truth, it's a God-shaped void."

His face showed his confusion as he said, "A God-shaped void?"

"Yeah," she continued. "That hole in your soul can only be filled by God, by asking Jesus Christ to come into your life and make you whole. I know you don't want to hear this. I didn't either, but I'm so glad that the lady that told this to me years ago didn't give up on me just because I didn't want to hear it. Really, Chris, my life has never been the same. I would NEVER go back to who I was before. She was an unhappy person and I would never be her again."

He thought for a long time. She grew silent, waiting for him to speak again. She didn't want to disturb his thoughts but knew he'd say something in his own time.

Soon he said softly, "I don't know. I've been a pretty bad character...for a lot of years. I'm too far gone."

She shook her head and continued softly, "Chris, it doesn't work that way. Listen, I know how bad you've been. Remember? Your life is written up in every magazine there is, and I've read it all."

He smiled but looked down, embarrassed. "You don't have to be ashamed in front of me," she said. "I've read about your life, but you've had no opportunity or reason to read about mine. Do you think you've got the market cornered on being bad?" He looked at her, surprised.

"You? Bad?"

"Of course," she answered.

"You don't seem like you could ever do anything bad!" he said.

"Well, believe me, what you see now is the new improved Holly, but I still mess up. The old Holly wasn't such pleasant company. See, when a person invites Jesus Christ to be in control, He accepts you just the way you are, warts and all, but He loves you too much to leave you that way. Look, I know you don't have children, but try to imagine this: if you had a child, and that child was bad for a long time, do you think you would ever give up on the kid coming around one day? Would you ever turn your back on your *kid*? Would there be a day when you would say, 'Okay, enough. I don't want to be around you anymore. Get out of my sight!' I don't think so. Maybe, but I don't think so. And God doesn't do that. He knows you and He loves you. He created you and He wants to spend time with you. He wants to help you live your life right. He can forgive you for any sin you've ever committed except the sin of not asking Him to forgive you! He can't forgive you until you ask...and then it's free. It's a free gift. I've already told you how to get the free gift, remember? Tell Him you know you're a sinner, ask His forgiveness, and ask Jesus Christ to come in and save you and make you whole. I'm telling you, you won't believe the new you. I still have a hard time believing I'm a new me sometimes, and it's been more than 20 years."

"You sound so confident, like it's the only way," he commented, looking down.

"Well, Chris, it *is* the only way. It says so in the Bible. Jesus said, 'I am the way, the truth, and the life. No man comes to the Father but by Me.' The world doesn't want to believe that, and I'm not sure why. It's the easiest option to me. I think of all the stuff other lines of thought suggest and it's all garbage to me. Like earning your way to Heaven? Okay, how good do I have to be? And by whose standard? Buddha's? Scientology's? The Mormons'? The Jehovah's Witnesses'? The New Age's? I can't be good enough to live up to man's standard because man will always hold me to something he has created, and man *himself* is imperfect. I can't be good enough to stand up under God's standard because His standard is perfection, but the thing is that God *knows* I can't measure up to His standard and accepts me for it. But He also gives me His guidance, which is also perfect. I can always trust Him. Who else can you ALWAYS trust? Do you know anyone that you think you can always trust? I don't! You think I'm Little Miss Perfect, but I'm telling you, you can't always trust me either. I will fail you at some point, not on purpose, but because I'm human. Please, Chris, don't make life harder for yourself than it has to be. I care about you, and I don't want to see you go to Hell. It's a real place. People don't like to believe it, but it's real. Jesus tells about it in the Bible...and He doesn't paint a pretty picture. Heaven, on the other hand? Now that's a masterpiece and I want you there with me and my family."

He studied her eyes and could tell she was sincere. She was looking him straight in the eye and had such a pained looked on her face, as if she may cry at any minute. "You're really serious, aren't you?" he asked.

"Dead serious," she answered, still looking him in the eye. "Please, Chris, won't you think hard about it?"

He met her gaze and said, "Well, what have I got to lose?"

She looked down at the ground and said, "Eternity, if you make the wrong choice," then looked back into his eyes and smiled weakly.

He stood up and walked around for awhile with his hands in his pockets and his head down. He walked the fifty feet or so over to the end of the fence and leaned on it with his forearms, staring at the ground for a long time. She remained seated, praying for him to come to Jesus and glancing at him occasionally. After awhile he walked back over to the bench, sat down and asked, "What if I try this and it doesn't work?"

She laughed and said, "It's not some magic formula. It doesn't work or not work. It's a heart thing. See, when you ask Jesus to come into your life, it's not because it's something you check off on a list of steps to freedom or anything like that. It's a matter of the heart...you come to Him because you know it's the right thing. Coming to Jesus is the start of a relationship, not a religion...and God knows your heart. He knows whether you're sincere when you ask Him into your life." She stopped for a moment then said, "The only way it won't 'work,'" as she made quotation marks in the air with her fingers, "is if you're not sincere in the first place."

He looked around, took his hat off, and ran his fingers through his chestnut hair. It was the first time his head had been uncovered in her presence, and she felt for some reason that this was another show of his trust in her as a friend. She felt as if God had drawn him closer to the goal. The scripture came to her mind again: *John 6:44–No one can come to Me unless the Father Who sent Me draws him, and I will raise him up at the last day.*

Finally he said, "Okay. I'm going to think about this tonight after I get back to my room." His attitude and demeanor seemed to change, as if he had taken a step toward a decision. He sighed then, as if a switch had been turned on, said, "I'm in the mood for ice cream. How about it?"

She marveled that he could go from one mood to another so quickly and easily. *After all, he is an actor,* she thought, but somehow she doubted that this was an act.

"You buying?" she asked as she gathered her things.

"If you'll let me," he came back, gathering his.

"All righty then," she said, standing up quickly.

He put on his hat and sunglasses, jumped to his feet and said, "Beat'cha there!"

"Dragging a shopping bag?! I don't think so!" she laughed.

"Okay, then. We'll just trudge down the rocky road."

"Ugh! That joke is straight out of Vaudeville!" she snapped, and they laughed as they walked the short distance to the corner where they had earlier passed an ice cream shop.

CHAPTER SEVEN

Cups of ice cream in hand, they talked between bites as they walked back toward their hotels. It was good to be in a lighthearted mood again.

"Are you excited about your trip back to Atlanta tomorrow?" he asked, wiping his napkin across his chin to catch the chocolate drip.

"You know, I really am," she admitted. "I can't believe I'm saying that, but I am."

"Sometimes the airlines change flights on you. Your plans still on for your flight?"

"Yeah. I called this morning to check. It's still a 'go,'" she said. She seemed deep in thought and far away. He didn't notice at first, but when she remained quiet for awhile, he saw that she wasn't eating her double dip of vanilla but just walking along holding it in her hand.

"It's melting," he said as he pointed to her cup.

"Huh? Oh, yeah. I guess I'm finished with it," she said as she turned around and tossed it into a nearby trash can.

"Something wrong?" he asked as she joined him again.

"Well," she started, "I think I'm a little sad. I've had such a good time...so much better than I thought I'd have, and I sorta hate to leave, although I'm anxious to get back home. You know, one of those bittersweet feelings...want to go home but hate to leave."

"Yeah, I know what you mean," he agreed.

"So when are you leaving?" she asked as she shifted her shopping bag to the other hand.

"Who knows? Still haven't had my R and R," he said with a grin.

Just then they arrived in front of The Crimson Tulip. "Well, I promised you I would do some thinking, and I'm a man of my word, so I guess I'll say goodbye and go to my room to meditate on it all." She smiled slightly, biting her lip and trying to hold back the tears. Another bittersweet moment...she'd had such a good time, but he hadn't accepted Jesus. She held out hope that he would, though, at some point. She also knew that when he did, she would find out because it would be in all the magazines, eventually. And they'd tear him to shreds. The mocking, the ridicule. She dreaded it. He held out his hand to shake hers then noticed her eyes filling with tears. "What's wrong?" he asked quietly. She shook her head and tried to compose herself.

"I feel like I'm losing a good friend," she said, tears streaming. He gave her a quick hug then stepped back.

"Me, too." He wasn't sure what to say then added, "You know, we have e-mail," he said, hoping it would comfort her.

"That's right. I forgot about that," she said, seeming to brighten a little. "So let's keep in touch, okay?" she asked with a hopeful look.

"Certainly," he replied.

He seemed like such an emotional type that she was a little surprised that he wasn't showing it very much now. The silence became awkward, and she said, "Well, I'll see you later. Bye."

"Okay. Bye-bye," he replied.

She walked to the hotel entrance, stopped and waved, then entered. He waved and turned toward the Adell. He strode through the revolving door and toward the elevators then went into the gift shop, looked at the packs of cigarettes, had no desire for them, then turned, entered the elevator, and went to his suite.

Remembering his promise to think about their conversation in the park, he started to get comfortable in the wing-back but decided to first check his e-mail, so he sat down at the desk, turned on his laptop and connected to the internet, clicking into his e-mail account. He deleted the junk and responded to a couple of short messages, then he noticed an e-mail from Holly. The subject line said, "This should help as you think." He clicked onto it and began reading:

These should help you as you begin thinking about our conversation. If there's not an English language Bible in your room, you can do a search for online Bibles and look them up there. You may not want to hear this, but I'm praying for you...that you'll discover what you're looking for.

See ya some day, I hope. Holly

John 3:16, John 14:6, Romans 3:23, Romans 6:23, Acts 26:18, Romans 5:12, Ephesians 2:8-9, John 1:12-13, I John 5:12-13

He sat still for a minute or two, uncomfortable with the idea of trying to read a Bible. His grandfather had been a fire-and-brimstone preacher when Chris was a child and had insisted that Chris read the Bible but had given him no instruction, no guidance...just told him to "go home, boy, and read your Bible." He had tried to read it but had gotten nowhere with it. How was it going to be any different now?

Nevertheless, he went to the drawer but found only a dog-eared phone book, so he went back to the computer and did a search for "online Bible," found several sites and clicked on the first hit. He found that he could search two versions at once and clicked on that option. After a quick scan of the many versions available, he chose the King James Version and the New American Standard, his logic for the first choice being that he had actually heard of the King James Version, and for the second, he was an American. He found all the passages easily and read them carefully. Some of them sounded a little scary but still he was interested. Somehow he felt drawn to them. He read them all again then went to the wing-back and settled in to think.

The confusion of the entertainment world's ideas about God clouded his mind, but the longer he sat and thought, the more he could remember about things he had heard about sin, not only from his grandfather, but from others. He had believed it was real then, but living in Hollywood and New York had caused him to push it so far away from him that he hadn't really thought about it in years. He was remembering...a lot...and was beginning to feel the guilt of so many years of drugs, alcohol, women, bad language, bad attitudes, and a host of other sins, and about how he had told Holly that he had been bad for so long that he was too far gone. What had she said? *Nothing could be further from the truth,* he recalled...and he remembered her eyes, so sincere. She had said that she knew him, that she had read a lot about him. Why, then, was she not repulsed at spending time with him? *After all, she's a Christian,* he thought. *Why wouldn't she feel dirty spending more than two minutes with someone like me?*

He felt himself beginning to be drawn to what she had said...all of it. He was amazed at how much he could remember of her discourse on the plane. He thought for a long time. It all really did make sense and he thought about how great it would feel to be free of all the guilt, the guilt that he had only just remembered because it had been suppressed for so long. He realized, though, that he had always known it was there and that he had lied when, in interview after interview, he had told reporters how happy he was. True freedom was what he really wanted...not freedom from his work or from any one person, but freedom of the soul. But he was scared. *Of what?* he asked himself in amazement. *I'm not scared of anything or anybody!* He thought on that, too, and finally realized that he was afraid of what he might have to give up, what might be required of him, of living a totally different life, a life he wasn't used to, of the rejection that would most assuredly attack him from all directions. Thinking about it any more tonight was something he just wasn't willing to do, and he turned off the computer and started preparing for bed. Chris really didn't think he'd sleep very much, but he just couldn't think any more tonight. He picked up the snow globe, pausing to give it one more turn, then packed it with the few things he had brought with him, placed them by the door, and went to bed. Oddly enough, he drifted peacefully to sleep.

Holly stopped by the gift shop and picked up a newspaper in the Dutch language, a souvenir for herself, to keep as a reminder of her victorious trip, a fear-conquering, soul-winning (eventually, she hoped) trip. She dropped it onto the bed and collected her things, packing them into her luggage and leaving out only the essentials to groom for tomorrow's flight. She stared out the window for awhile as she reminisced about her brief stay in Amsterdam. What a trip this had been! Not at all as she had expected, from beginning to end. *Well, almost the end. Guess we'll see how the trip goes tomorrow,* she mused. She basked in her feelings of victory, happiness, and obedience, although it was still painful to think that Chris was lost and it would be a long time, and many magazines and news stories, before she would know whether her witness had born fruit.

She went down for a snack then returned to her room and, after awhile, prepared for bed. As she settled under the covers, she thanked God for His mercy and love, His sovereignty and might, His patience and compassion, still unable to fathom, after all these years, how He could love her so much. Within minutes she fell asleep, dreaming of a calm flight home, reading a book about the comedic greats.

Chris awoke from a dead sleep to the sound of sirens and slowly sat up, wondering if he were dreaming. No, those were definitely sirens. Were they at the Adell? He squinted at the clock by his bed. Three-thirty. Still groggy, he stumbled to the picture window that faced the street and saw the flashing lights of two police cars next door at The Crimson Tulip. The sirens stopped but the lights continued to flash as two more cruisers screeched to a stop in front of the hotel and more officers ran to its entrance, guns drawn, as they slammed their backs against the stone and brick edifice beside one set of revolving doors. Suddenly he heard two shots pierce the night! They came from inside the hotel!

His eyes widened. *What's going on?* Senses awakening, he remembered his new friend. *Holly!* He ran for the phone book in the night stand drawer and fumbled with the pages until he found the phone number for The Crimson Tulip, knowing his efforts were useless. He quickly dialed the number. No answer. It wouldn't even ring. The phone system was jammed with calls. *Stupid! Why didn't you get her cell phone number?* Frustrated with himself, he paced the floor, running long fingers through his bed head, wondering if she was all right and trying to come up with some way to find out. "What's happening over there?" he wondered aloud. Running out into the night could get him killed, but fear of the unknown was eating him alive. He paced. His many roles involving police work and the criminal element raced through his mind. *So this is what it's **really** like.*

A hopeful thought occurred to him. *She wouldn't try to contact me, would she? You don't suppose...* He ran to his computer and rushed through the steps to connect to his e-mail account. "Inbox, 1 message." He was breathing in short pants as he quickly clicked on it and read:

"Chris, I'm all right. I don't know what's going on, but I'm all right. Don't worry." He was amazed.

It's like she knew I'd nut up if I didn't hear from her! He checked the time of the message. Three-thirty-five. He hit reply and quickly typed, "I heard shots! Stay in your room! Don't sign off...stay with me!" then hit "send" and left his e-mail up, returning to the window. Nothing was happening. No sound. No movement. Three musical notes came from his computer. "Inbox, 1 message." He clicked.

"Okay, I'm still here."

Grateful that they now had an ongoing connection, he calmed but only slightly. He knew they'd never let anyone in or out of the building for hours, but he had to keep watch. He wouldn't go back to bed till he knew the hotel was safe again. Oddly, he felt he owed that to Stephen Monroe.

All of a sudden an ambulance screamed to the hotel entrance and two attendants hurriedly opened the back, produced a stretcher, and ran into the hotel, using its only stationary door. Chris waited in silence. Within 15 minutes they hurried back out, hoisted the gurney into the ambulance, and sped away. It appeared to Chris that the person on the gurney was a woman, but he was too far away to make out details. As Chris continued to watch, two policemen emerged from the hotel with a man in handcuffs and loaded him into the back seat of the first patrol car.

Chris went back to his computer, quickly typed a report of what he had seen, hit "send," and waited for Holly's reply. Within seconds he breathed a sigh of relief as he read her message.

"I was so scared. Do you think it's over?" He went back to the window and saw that only one patrol car was left. Chris was a very conscientious actor, so he researched the minutest details of each part he played. From his research for police roles he had played, he knew that the officers from that car were inside taking statements from witnesses. He relayed this information to her, they communicated for awhile then decided that they should try and sleep but not until they had exchanged cell phone numbers, Chris, naturally, telling her that his was a private number. Of course, this was not news to her.

They were both actually able to fall asleep relatively quickly and catch a few more hours' sleep until they needed to be up and ready for the next day.

A few hours later he awoke completely surprised that he had slept any more at all, not only because of the previous night's commotion, but also because of his turbulent emotions, and fear and uneasiness at any thought of Jesus.

CHAPTER EIGHT

After Holly stowed her carry-on, she took seat G1 next to the window. Although she trusted that she was over her fear of flying, she was still amazed that she felt no apprehension, no uneasiness, no fear. Jesus had answered her prayer for deliverance from that fear, and it was a wonderful feeling, a freedom she had not known in over 25 years. It would be quite a testimony some day, she hoped, and she would give God all the glory, thanking Him for putting Chris Lapp in the seat beside her to help her through the pain. That would be a story for her grandchildren some day. She marveled at how God uses unsaved people. How she hoped that some day she would read that he had become a Christian, not just a marginal Christian, but a man who would really live for the Lord the life He called him to, a life that would lead others to Jesus Christ. She stared out the window, lost in thought, unaware of the airport workers readying the plane for the transatlantic flight...not even aware of the man with a newspaper who had taken his seat next to her in F1. She was oblivious to his presence, or anything else for that matter. He folded his paper and placed it in the back of his portfolio, which was lying in his lap. He studied her for a long time, wondering what had her so mesmerized. He fell pensive and opened the portfolio to a clean white sheet, retrieving his pencil and drawing careful, perfect lines, clearly the work of a talented artist. He finished the piece, replaced the pencil and closed the portfolio, satisfied with his work.

He looked at Holly again...she hadn't moved since he had boarded. He was wondering if he should say something to her, but just then he heard the engines rev and the plane began to taxi into position for takeoff. The movement interrupted Holly's thoughts. She straightened up in her seat noticing that the seat next to her was no longer vacant and was amazed that she had been so preoccupied that she had not noticed her seat mate. She only gave him a casual glance then noticed dirt on her shoe and leaned down to brush it away. As she did, a familiar sight caught her eye...the shoes. She stopped and quickly turned to her right, looking up to see his face, but he had turned to his right, hand on his cheek. She sat back up and studied his clothes...jeans are jeans, so she looked at his shirt, hat, and sunglasses but didn't recognize them. Then she looked back at his shoes. Confused, she looked back out the window then back at him and down at his shoes and back out the window. By now he was stifling a laugh. Knowing he couldn't hold out much longer, he faced forward and calmly removed his sunglasses with the hand that was hiding his cheek. When she looked back at him again, she gasped loudly and he looked her squarely in the eye, a big grin covering his face.

"It can't be!" she exclaimed almost too loudly. Fortunately, they had front seats, and the seats directly behind and beside them were empty. Realizing how loud she had been, she looked around and lowered her voice. "Chris! It's you!" she almost whispered, in an attempt to conceal his identity from the other passengers.

"Yeah," he said, nodding his head and still flashing the big grin.

"What...how...when?" She couldn't make a complete sentence.

"Breathe!" he said, laughing.

She took a deep breath. "You bought a new disguise!"

"Well, I couldn't buy new cheekbones, so I had to settle for a new hat and shades!"

"Why didn't you tell me you were flying back today?" she asked him, still in disbelief.

"'Cause I wanted to surprise you," he replied.

"You mean you had this planned the whole time? How did you do that?" she asked.

"Well, no, I only planned it yesterday as we left the ice cream shop. It was really hard, too, because you seemed so sad," he said with a pained face. "You were pretty pitiful. It was all I could do to keep from giving away the whole secret when you started to cry outside The Crimson Tulip. I felt awful after you went inside the hotel."

She laughed and said, "Well, I wondered why you seemed to be almost totally unemotional about the whole thing."

"Believe me, I wasn't," was his reply as he became more serious. He looked at her, trying to decide if saying what he was about to say was the right thing to do. "I don't want you to take this the wrong way because I don't mean it the way it's gonna sound, but there's something about you. Something about your personality, your whole being, that I want."

Scarlett O'Hara spoke again, "Please, Mr. Lapp," she gushed, making two syllables out of "Lapp." "You're goin' to make me blush," and she tossed her head.

He said, "No, silly, that's not what I mean."

She became serious again and said, "I know it's not. In fact, I know exactly what you mean...and what you're seeing is Christ in me. What you want has nothing to do with me and everything to do with Jesus."

With a confused look, he said, "What? I don't get it."

She laid her head back against the headrest for a moment then looked at him and said, "You know lots of people, right?" He nodded. "How many of them are Christians, that you know of?"

He thought a few seconds then said, "I don't think any of them are."

"Are you drawn to any of them the way you're drawn to me?"

He shook his head, "Oddly enough, I don't think so."

"I'm just going to be brutally blunt here...the draw isn't sexual, is it?"

"Nah, girls are available any time I want," he said with a matter-of-fact shrug. "There's an honesty about you, though. You're real, you're not a fake."

Holly looked down and smiled. "Good," she said. "That's the way it's supposed to be. Christians aren't supposed to be fake...about anything." By now the plane had been in the air for a few minutes, and the conversation turned from one thing to another including the events of the previous night. Chris filled her in on what he had heard and seen and asked if she had any information on what had actually occurred. She explained that the man was a transient in need of money and simply thought he could walk into the hotel and take all he wanted. "Yeah, it appears he forgot this little thing called the law," she quipped. "He also shot the desk clerk, but they say she's going to be all right."

He sat quietly for awhile, then she asked him, "How did the meditation go last night?"

"Meditation?"

"Yeah, you know. You were going to meditate on our conversation in the park yesterday?"

"Oh, yeah. Well," he began, "I looked up all the verses you told me to and read them...twice...and thought about them a long time. It brought back to mind a lot of stuff I remembered hearing when I was younger...stuff I'd forgotten."

"Stuff?" she wondered aloud.

"Yeah, stuff about sin and death and about how Jesus can take care of all that," he answered.

"Good stuff," she said. "Important stuff. Decision-making stuff."

Just then his stomach growled, and they both laughed. "Guess it's time to eat," he said.

"Perfect timing," she said as the flight attendant appeared with their meal, which they ate as they talked about what they planned to do when they each arrived home. He was ready for lighthearted conversation again and asked about her family and how they had gotten along while she had been away.

"Oh, I've talked with them several times and they seem to be fine. Ready for me to come home and tell them all about my trip. Of course, what they really want to hear about are the plane rides. I'm glad I'll be able to give a good report."

"Do they know you've been traveling with a buddy?" he asked as he took a drink from his bottle of water. What he really wanted to know was whether she had told them who her traveling buddy was, but he didn't want to appear egotistical.

She grinned and said, "I haven't told them I'm traveling with Chris Lapp, if that's what you mean." He shyly looked down and opened his bag of chips.

They munched their food hungrily for a minute, then Chris asked, "Would it be too much of an imposition if I met your family? They're picking you up at the airport, aren't they?"

"You want to meet my family?" she asked. "Why would you want to do that?"

He shrugged. "I have no idea, but I do," was his reply.

"Well, of course, it would be fine. It wouldn't be an imposition at all. And don't worry, they won't flip out or anything like that." He laughed and said that somehow he didn't think they would. "Are you gonna tell them what a cry baby I was?" she queried, laughing but looking disgusted.

"I wasn't going to do that at all," he answered a little surprised.

"Well, if you don't I probably will," she retorted, still laughing. "I'll tell them the whole thing. They'll get a charge out of it."

The rest of the flight was spent napping, eating lunch and talking about their childhoods, hers in the mill villages of north Georgia and his in the coal mining towns of Pennsylvania. He even told her about his fire-and brimstone-preaching grandfather, whom Chris had only spent small amounts of time with due to his nomadic childhood.

"Yeah, I know what you mean. They mean well, but I always wondered why the preacher told us that Jesus loved us and then yelled about Him. That was the way it was back then, though." She paused a moment then said, "I loved those dear men, but I prefer the pleasant ones who seem genuinely happy and want to share with me the truths of the Bible without screaming and sweating. I guess there's a place for that, but it's just not my preference."

"I guess," he said with a faraway look, lovingly remembering his grandfather but wondering why he couldn't have been easier to talk to and why he had not been allowed more time with him.

Holly looked at her watch and said, "We should be landing in about half an hour or so. I'm anxious to see my family."

Chris said, "I bet you are. I'm looking forward to meeting them."

She said, "They'll be so surprised. Maybe we'll find you a spot in the shadows to stand until I give them a heads up that they're going to be meeting you. That way they'll keep a low profile so you won't be recognized."

"Sounds a like a plan."

The sky was beautiful as they circled the airport in Atlanta for a landing. White puffy clouds as far as the eye could see. Holly breathed a contented sigh as she thought about the events of the past couple of days and tried to imagine her family's faces as they met Christopher Terrence Lapp, Jr.

The plane made a smooth-as-silk landing, and the passengers deplaned. Holly and Chris walked to the luggage carousel with their things, Holly looking for her family and Chris looking for a spot to stand out of the way so that she could prepare her family to meet him. She soon spotted her husband, children and son-in-law walking toward her. She ran to them and they all embraced in a group hug. They were very excited for her and wanted to hear all about her trip and how she had handled the flights, but she asked if she could tell them all about it over dessert.

All this time Chris was standing in his place in the shadows watching and smiling, wishing he had a family to meet him with open arms. He noticed Holly's family stood still and was listening to her as she seemed to be explaining something. Then they all quietly turned and looked in his direction then back at her. A couple of eyebrows raised, a couple of mouths dropped open, but no one made a scene. Rose said it didn't look like him, and Holly explained that he was more recognizable in America, so he had to be more careful and wear a disguise. As Chris watched the exchange, he breathed a sigh of relief, knowing she had told them he was there, then he noticed them calmly approaching. Holly drew them all closely together so she could introduce them quietly.

"Christopher Lapp, I'd like you to meet my family," she addressed him as she pointed to each one, calling them by name. "This is my husband, Stephen Monroe, our son, Keith, and our daughter and son-in-law, Rose and Michael Bowdon." They all shook hands and said they were glad to meet one another, then Stephen invited them all for dessert, including Chris, who accepted graciously. They went to the luggage carousel, found their luggage and followed her family to the parking garage where they found the red SUV, piled all their things and themselves in and discussed where to go for dessert.

"Well," Holly began, "we all like ice cream and there's an ice cream specialty restaurant close by. It's late, so it won't be crowded and we can sneak Chris in under his disguise so no one will know it's him. How does that sound?" Everyone agreed, so they drove a couple of miles, found the place, went in, were seated with no trouble, and placed their orders. The conversation was light and cheerful with Holly's family asking all kinds of questions about her trip and the flights. She and Chris told them all about the flight over, the day of tulips and cheese, the shooting scare at the hotel, and the flight back. They fielded several questions, especially about the shooting, then Holly brought out a small bag from her purse and announced that she had brought souvenirs for everyone, over which they all "oohed" and "aahed."

Then Chris announced that he, too, had a gift to present... to Holly. She looked shocked and wondered aloud what it could be. He quietly drew out his portfolio and extracted a beautiful pencil drawing of Holly. The resemblance was uncanny, and they all said so. "Chris," she said weakly through the tears. "It's beautiful," she breathed. "I saw you drawing something on the flight over to Amsterdam, but I didn't allow myself to peek over your shoulder. Was it this?"

He said, "Well, I started drawing one then, but I put it away after awhile. It just didn't feel right...it also didn't look right. There was something about it that just, well, it was just off a bit, and I didn't know why. Then when I got on the plane this morning and you didn't notice me for so long, I was able to study your face and I knew that was the picture I wanted. You looked so content...there were no lines of fear on your face. It was so serene...even though you were in another world, you looked so peaceful."

Michael pointed to something in the picture and asked, "What's that in her hair?"

Chris smiled and said, almost in a whisper, "I wondered if anybody was going to ask. Those are wings. Holly got her wings. She can fly again."

Everyone was quiet for a long time as she looked at it and cried. They all knew the tears were tears of joy, not just for the picture but for what it represented...healing and deliverance from a load of baggage that had weighed her down for an eternity. It was gone forever...and she was so happy... happier than she had been in years. God had delivered her from this monstrous burden.

CHAPTER NINE

The server brought Stephen the check and Chris started to raise an arm. Holly looked at him with eyebrows raised and lips tight. He lowered his arm and said, "Yes, ma'am." Everyone else gave them inquisitive looks.

She laughed and said, "Thank you. It's time you let someone do something nice for you for a change." She explained to her family about Chris's generosity in picking up tabs on the trip.

"Something nice for *me*?" he asked in surprise. "All she did was something nice for me on the entire trip!" he told the others. "She let me tag along on the tulip and cheese trip, she talked with me about God, she encouraged me in a lot of ways." He laughed a little and said, "She let me pay for things."

"Yeah, he really had to twist my arm," Holly laughed. Her family thought that amusing.

"Well, I'm full," Rose sighed, "and it looks like they'd like to close up shop here."

Keith added, "Yeah, we should leave, I guess."

Chris asked, "Would it be okay if I got a picture with you all before we leave?"

Stephen said, "Sure. Where's your camera? In the car?"

"Yeah, it's in my small bag." They all rose and headed out to the car where Chris retrieved his camera.

Stephen whistled and said, "Nice one." He inspected it quickly and said, "It has a timer on it. Bet we can put it on top of the car and get us all in one shot. That way we won't have to find someone to take the picture and we can all still be in it. Everybody line up...you know the drill, tallest in the back, shortest in the front. Save a spot for me on the back." They all quickly grouped together, Stephen set up the shot, set the timer and took his place in the group. After the flash went off, Stephen gave Chris the camera and they all loaded back into the SUV.

"Where are you staying tonight, Chris?" asked Stephen. "We'll be glad to drop you off."

Silence. "Well, I feel stupid," was Chris's answer as he rolled his eyes and shook his head.

"What about?" Keith asked.

Chris said, "I was concentrating so much on pulling the surprise on Holly and looking forward to meeting you folks that I completely forgot to make a reservation here in Atlanta."

They all laughed then Keith said, "Is there any reason you can't stay with us tonight? Is that okay, Mom?"

"Well, sure it is," Holly answered.

"Oh, no, no. I couldn't do that," Chris insisted.

"And why not? Our house not good enough for you?" Stephen teased.

"I just couldn't. That would be too much of an imposition on you," Chris answered.

Holly looked at Stephen and cautiously said, "Wait a minute...what does the house look like?"

He laughed and answered, "I think you'll be pleasantly surprised."

Keith leaned over and said, "We cleaned."

"You cleaned?" she asked in feigned horror. "Well, Chris, you *have* to come and stay with us now...I wouldn't want you to miss this. They cleaned!" Everyone laughed and agreed that he should make the three-hour trip to Wells with them and stay a few days, so he finally gave in.

"Holly, your family is just as great as you said they are," Chris told her.

They rode along through the night making conversation for the first couple of hours, then everyone began to yawn. Chris and Keith fell asleep in the back seat while Rose and Michael snoozed in the middle seat. Stephen and Holly held hands and caught up on tidbits of news from Wells and talked more about Holly's trip.

"I had a really nice time, but the best part is that God delivered me from my fear of flying. I could very easily go back to the airport and get on another plane right now bound for who-knows-where, anywhere. He is so good."

"I'm really happy for you, honey," Stephen said, glancing lovingly at her. "I can't wait till you and I can take a plane trip together somewhere. It's been so long."

"Yeah, I know. Me, too," she answered in the same low tone.

At last they turned onto the street where Rose and Michael lived and woke the nappers. They drove into the driveway and as Rose and Michael got out, Stephen said, "See you tomorrow at 4:00?"

"Yeah, looking forward to it," Rose replied

"Goodnight," Chris told them.

"Goodnight," they replied as they sleepily dragged themselves into their house, barely waving as they shut the door behind them.

Part of the conversation along the way had included plans for a cookout the next day for just the six of them. Everyone had promised not to tell anyone that Chris was in town so that he wouldn't be bombarded by autograph seekers and rubberneckers. This was to be a time of relaxation for them all. Holly hoped it would be more...that Chris would see how a mature Christian family functions and that maybe he would realize that he wanted and needed Jesus.

"Guest room look okay?" Holly asked as they drove into the garage.

"Better than when you left," Keith said proudly. They gathered all their things and went inside.

"Great to be home," Holly said with a yawn.

"Great to be in *your* home," Chris said.

"Keith, you want to show Chris to the guest room and show him where the towels are?"

"Sure," Keith answered. "This way," he said as he motioned for Chris to follow him.

"Let's all make a pact," Holly said as Keith and Chris left the room. "Let's all agree to sleep until we wake up. No alarms or anything."

"You don't have to tell *me* twice," Chris said. "I think I'm going to sleep better here than I have in many nights."

Everyone went to bed and the house was quiet. As Holly kissed Stephen goodnight and relaxed on her own bed, she said, "Bet I wake up in the morning and this is all a dream." Then she closed her eyes.

Holly awoke the next morning and looked at the clock. "Eleven o'clock?!" she said out loud. She looked toward Stephen's side of the bed, but he wasn't there. Then she smelled bacon and knew he had gotten up and was cooking a most scrumptious breakfast. Or maybe at this hour it was brunch. She quickly got up, hopped in the shower and dressed. "I love this haircut," she said to herself. "Don't have to do a thing to it except brush it."

She went to the kitchen and found her thoughtful husband putting the finishing touches on a lavish breakfast. "What's this?" she asked as she kissed him and smiled.

"Probably the best breakfast this side of the Mississippi," Stephen answered with false pride.

"Uh-uh," she warned with a giggle. "Pride goes before a fall." Just then Keith and Chris came in through the back door from a walk around the neatly manicured yard.

"Good morning, Sleepyhead," Keith said as he kissed his mother.

"Good morning, darling," she answered with a smile.

"Good morning, Holly," Chris said.

"Good morning, Chris," Holly smiled again.

"Good morning, John-Boy. Good morning, Jim-Bob," Stephen added in a sing-song voice, breaking them all up.

"Your flowers are gorgeous," Chris complimented her, "but I was surprised to see there wasn't a single tulip."

She nodded sadly. "They don't do well in the Deep South," Holly explained. "You have to plant new bulbs yearly or dig them up every year and give them a false winter in the fridge for about six weeks before you finally plant them around January or February. Too much trouble, I guess."

"Oh, so you'd rather fly across the pond to The Netherlands to see them, huh?" he teased.

"Sure, why not?" was her comeback.

"Brunch is served," Stephen said with a British accent as he placed the last serving bowl on the dining room table and bowed butler-style, towel over his arm.

"Oh, thank you, Jeeves," Holly answered in a high-brow tone of voice as she moved toward her seat at the table.

As Keith took his regular seat Stephen motioned toward an empty chair and said, "Chris, that one's for you."

Holly peered at the table and said, "My goodness, honey. You outdid yourself this time."

Keith said, 'Yeah, Dad, it looks great," as he placed his napkin in his lap and reached for his juice glass.

Chris said, "Wow, I didn't know I was so hungry. This looks great."

Stephen was a good cook and had taught Holly a lot about cooking when they first married. She could open cans of food and heat them up and make scrambled eggs and toast, but that was the extent of her culinary prowess when they married more than 30 years earlier. Today Stephen had laid out a feast: scrambled eggs with toppings of shredded cheddar and jack cheeses and chives, grits to which cheeses could also be added, hash browns for Chris (since Stephen was unsure as to whether Chris had ever been introduced to the Southern favorite), huge fluffy pancakes, fried sausage patties with creamy sausage gravy, and homemade cat head biscuits. In Holly's little preserve dishes he had placed apple butter and grape and strawberry jams. Keith was partial to honey, so a little dish of honey was also included. Stephen had heated maple syrup and placed it in one of Holly's favorite pitchers from her collection. She loved glass things, especially Depression glass, and this small clear glass pitcher was one that her mother had told her about retrieving from an oatmeal box when she was a girl in the 1930's.

They all ate until they were full and declared they couldn't eat another bite. Holly stood and started clearing the table, but Keith said, "No, Mom. You relax. Dad and I will handle this."

Chris said, "I'd really like to help, if that's okay."

Stephen said, "No, no. You're our guest. In fact, when we have dinner guests, Holly won't do the dishes until later because she always wants to spend as much time as possible with whomever is visiting. Of course, when they're overnight guests, she does eventually have to see that the kitchen is put back in order." He turned to Holly and said, "But let Keith and me handle it this time. You and Chris go into the family room and relax. It'll probably be awhile before you're over the jet lag completely." She and Chris shrugged at each other and obeyed.

They strode into the large, comfortable family room and took seats opposite each other on the brown leather sofas that faced each other near the fireplace. "Too bad it's not a little cool. We could start a fire," Holly said gazing into the cold, empty fireplace. "It's always so peaceful in the wintertime when we can have a little blaze burning. I love to stare into it and daydream."

"Oh, yeah? And what do you daydream about?" Chris asked curious as to what she liked besides tulips and cheese.

"Well, I always dream about traveling to faraway places and seeing the sights." He nodded.

"Like where?"

She thought a moment then said, "Fiji, Tahiti, Samoa, Hawaii...any place where there's a beach and beautiful sand and water. And London, Rome, Paris, Madrid... and Amsterdam." She looked into the kitchen and caught Stephen's smiling face and smiled widely back.

He said, "You don't have to daydream about that one anymore."

"No, I don't, do I?" she laughed.

Chris smiled and said, "No. I can testify that you can strike that one off your list."

Keith came in and took a seat in his favorite chair, the green one with an ottoman. "So, Mom," he said winking at Chris, "where you off to now?"

She looked at him and frowned. "I've just gotten home and you're packing me off again?! Thanks a lot!"

"Well, I have the answer to that, if you'll accept it," Chris said folding his arms with a shrug.

"Well, don't you look all smug?" Holly asked curiously. "And what scheme have you concocted now?

"Well," he started, "do you remember when we were talking about traveling and I asked if you have friends who have places where you can stay?" She thought a minute then nodded expectantly. "Well, it just so happens that you do have a friend with a place, several places actually, all over the world." Holly glanced at Stephen who was drying his hands and walking toward the family room.

She said playfully, "Yeah? Who?"

He leaned up on his knees with his elbows and said, "Me. I have a place in Hawaii and a place in Paris and three other apartments scattered over New York, Los Angeles and Miami...and I want you and your family to know that you are welcome to stay in them whenever you want to, as long as no one else is there, which is hardly ever."

"Are you serious?" Keith asked, mouth dropping open.

"Wouldn't that be a lot of trouble to you?" asked Stephen, looking first at Chris and then at Holly and then back at Chris.

"Is it a lot of trouble having me here, especially unexpectedly like this?"

"Not at all!" Holly answered emphatically.

"Then 'Not at all' is my answer, too," Chris retorted, throwing his hands up in the air, leaning back against the couch and folding his hands behind his neck.

They all looked at each other a little dazed. "Well, when do we leave for Paris?!" Keith yelled, jumping up.

"Hold your horses, son," said Stephen. "There's this little matter of purchasing plane tickets, and..."

Chris interrupted with, "Uh, I also have a plane." They all looked at him with mouths open.

"You're offering us the use of your plane, too?" Holly breathed quietly.

"When I'm not using it," he answered, nodding.

She stood up and walked around the room. "This is too much," she said as she stopped at the window and pretended to watch a hummingbird at the feeder. A tear slipped from her eye and rolled down her cheek as she stood motionless at the window. No one said anything, and she knew they were all watching her. She finally was able to glance their way as she wiped the tear from her cheek and figured they deserved an explanation. "It's what I've always wanted...you know, to travel, to see far-off places. I just never expected to," she said softly as she walked back to the couch and sat down. "Oh, shoot, I need a tissue. I'll be right back," she said as she got up and slipped down the hall.

When she had disappeared and was out of earshot, Stephen spoke. "Listen, Chris, our anniversary is coming up in about a month or so..." he began.

"Don't say another word...would the villa in Paris be okay?"

CHAPTER TEN

As she came back down the hall, Chris put his finger to his lips and whispered, "We'll talk later," then asked louder, "What time is the cookout with Rose and Michael today?"

"Four o'clock," Holly answered as she plopped back down on the couch. "Are we changing the subject that quickly? I was sorta enjoying all the travel talk," she sheepishly admitted.

"Well, honey, we'll have to look at our calendars and make plans and call Chris and, well, you know, all that technical stuff," Stephen said, then he turned to Chris and changed the subject by saying, "You know, we haven't even exchanged phone numbers and addresses."

Holly chimed in, "We've exchanged e-mail addresses! And already used them! I sent Chris some scriptures one night on the trip."

"Then there was this little matter of a hotel robbery when we kept cyberspace burning for awhile," Chris added.

Just then the phone rang. It was Rose. "Hey, Mom. We still coming at four?"

"Yeah, unless that's not good."

"Oh, no, no. That's fine. Would you like me to bring something?"

"Yeah, how about some of your killer baked beans to go with the hamburgers and hot dogs?"

"You got it!"

"And some of your homemade lemonade?"

"Okay. Anything else?"

"No, honey, that'll do it, I think."

"Okay. See ya then."

"If you're ready before four, just come on over."

"Okay. 'Bye."

"'Bye, baby."

"Speaking of e-mail, I think I'll check mine," Keith announced and headed for his room.

"You folks really love your kids, don't you?" Chris asked. "I mean, you're a really tightly knit family, aren't you?

"Oh, yes. Why do you ask?" answered Holly.

"It's just obvious. I mean, besides calling them 'baby' and stuff like that, it's just obvious. Your 24-year-old daughter wanted to meet you at the airport, and the boy is 20 years old and enjoys sitting around talking with his parents."

"Both our kids have always been that way. Not that there weren't some rough places along the way but we always talked with them, included them in our conversations, tried to have meals together and talk about whatever came to mind. We've always kept the lines of communication open, always told them they could talk with us...about anything." Holly giggled then added, "And sometimes the conversation was, well, REALLY interesting. They asked us about stuff we never dreamed they'd ask us about, but we always told them the truth. A kid can tell if he's being had or if you're on the level."

"Yeah, and we always encouraged them to do things outside of church and school, like playing ball and getting into music, you know, stuff like that. And we were always at their games and concerts and plays and whatever they were into. They need to know that Mom and Dad are interested," Stephen elaborated. He waited a minute then said, "You know, there were kids on the ball teams and in the band and chorus whose parents we never saw at any of the functions. It was sad, really."

Chris was quiet, lost in thought, remembering his own childhood when times were tough and all he could do was hang around with his friends, usually the wrong kinds of friends. He desperately wanted to be involved in other things but didn't have the encouragement or the money. From the blank stare on his face, Holly and Stephen could see that he was in another world and quietly waited for him to speak again. Soon he looked up and saw that they were waiting for him, so he said, "Oh, sorry. I was just thinking about what that might have been like. My childhood wasn't quite like Keith's and Rose's." He shook it off and jumped up and said, "Okay, enough of that stuff."

Stephen seized the opportunity and said, "How about a walk around the neighborhood, Chris? Sometimes I do that to stretch my legs before I'm gonna be standing on 'em for awhile...like when I'm grilling burgers and dogs."

"Okay. I was getting a little fidgety anyway," Chris answered.

"We'll be back in time for me to start the grill," Stephen said with a wink as he and Chris walked through the kitchen and started for the back door. "Pray for us," he mouthed to Holly when Chris had gone out the door. She nodded with an understanding look.

"Oh, God," she began as she watched them walk down the long driveway toward the quiet street. "You know my prayer is that Chris comes to Jesus Christ. Draw him, Lord, as Stephen speaks, and help Stephen to be sensitive to your Holy Spirit as he speaks to Chris. Work in that walk according to Your will. Thank You, Lord, for all that You're going to do in this. In Jesus' Name I pray, Amen."

She felt a quiet confidence as she left it with God and went about getting the kitchen ready to prepare her part of the evening meal. She glanced at the clock: 1:30. "Keith," she called out.

"Yeah, Mom?"

"Would you go to the store for the bread and meats?"

Keith appeared from his room and said, "Sure. You got mun?"

She smirked as she pulled a twenty from her purse in the laundry room. "Bring me the change."

"If there is any," he replied as he winked and opened the door to leave. She smiled as she shut the door behind him and turned to the joy of preparing a pecan pie. She loved to cook but especially loved to bake: cakes, pies, breads, cookies and the occasional fancy sweet roll. She made the crust (which would be so flaky...it always was) and put it into her mother's battered old pie pan. Then she pulled the worn recipe card from her recipe box and lovingly mixed the rich ingredients, carefully pouring the sweet concoction into the crust. She placed it in the hot oven, set the timer for 45 minutes and wiped her hands on her grandmother's apron that hung around her neck and tied at the waist. It was plain and white and had been meticulously fashioned from washed and bleached flour sacks. That's how things were done in the poor south early in the twentieth century. This apron was probably 75 years old, and Holly knew that using it as often as she did would probably wear it out, but she couldn't bear the thought of just packing it up and letting it dry rot. Grandmother McDonnell would certainly think that a waste. Grandmother had been a stately woman, tall and confident. Holly barely remembered her at all and probably only then because of pictures taken when Holly was three or four years old. Grandmother had died just before Holly's fifth birthday, and the apron had been passed down to Holly's precious mother, Lydia, a woman that Holly aspired to emulate. She had been Holly's inspiration all her life till she died in her 60's. It was because of Lydia's prayers that Holly had come to know Jesus Christ.

Keith returned with the bread and meats and handed Holly the change. "Thanks, honey. That saved me a lot of time," she said with a smile as he walked through the family room toward the hall.

"Sure thing, Mom." Holly put the meats in the refrigerator and breads on the island. Then she cleaned the counter top and unloaded the dishwasher, reloading it with the few dirty utensils she had used to make the pie. She cleaned the counter top again and rechecked the time: 2:20. She looked out the front window. No sign of them.

"God, I pray that it's going Your way," she prayed and smiled as she walked back into the kitchen. She finished getting things ready for Stephen to grill the food and retrieved two bags of chips from the freezer where she always kept spare bags of potato chips, just in case. Good thing because she had forgotten to add chips to her grocery list for Keith. She was known for being forgetful at times. It had been a joke for years. Fortunately, she usually remembered the important things, though.

"Keith! Frozen chips!" she called in a sing-song voice. In a flash she heard him running down the hall.

"Yesss!" he said as he grabbed a bag of barbecues and ripped it open. "Mmmm," he moaned as he crunched the cool, salty snack.

"Okay, that's enough," she said as she picked up the bag and rolled the top down. She finished her mouthful then opened the bag and said, "You and I are just alike. We can't stop once we start on these things," and she shoved a wad into her mouth. They crunched together for awhile then Holly put the bag away. "Save some for the others," she said, taking off the apron and draping it across the island as she retreated to the family room. Keith came along and plopped down on the couch beside her.

"Mom, what in the world did you think when you first saw Chris get on the plane?" he questioned with wide eyes and a big grin. "You didn't do anything embarrassing, did you?"

"No, in fact, you would have been really proud of me. God was SO good. I noticed Chris and then just kept my cool. I even pretended I didn't recognize him," she giggled.

"Does he know all this?" Keith asked, eyes still wide.

"Yeah, we talked and laughed about it on the flight home," she answered. "You know, he's such a nice guy. I really enjoyed getting to know him. He's not full of himself or arrogant like you'd think he'd be. But he really does need Jesus Christ in his life. I could tell that much of the time on the trip he was uneasy, unhappy. Oh, he had a good time, but there was just something unsettled about him. I've been praying for him regularly ever since he first sat down beside me on the plane. In fact, if you want to know a secret, Daddy is talking with him about the Lord right now." Keith's eyebrows raised. She said, "They've been gone about an hour. I'm itching to know how it's going."

"Then I think I'll go to my room and pray," Keith said, rising from the couch. "Back in a few minutes."

"That would be great, honey. Thanks." Keith went to his room and shut the door and Holly laid down on the couch and dropped off to sleep.

She woke to the sound of the door shutting in the kitchen. Rose and Michael were setting baked beans and lemonade on the counter. "You're early!" Holly said as she sat up on the couch. "Good! We can visit for awhile."

"Where is everybody?" Michael asked looking around. Keith is in his room and Daddy and Chris have gone for a walk. I think Daddy wanted to talk with him about spiritual things."

"Ooo, good. How long have they been gone?" Rose wondered aloud.

"Well, they left around 1:30," Holly answered. "Couple of hours, I guess. I can't wait till they get back." She got up and strode to the kitchen. "Have a seat. I'll be with you in a minute," she said as she turned off the beeping timer and peeked at the pie. It was done, so she removed it from the oven, turned it off, and placed the baked beans in to keep warm. After setting the lemonade in the refrigerator, she joined Rose and Michael in the family room and Keith walked in, settling down in his favorite chair.

"Mom, what did you think when you realized that Chris Lapp was going to be your seat mate to Amsterdam? Were you just beside yourself?" Rose asked, her face taking on a look of awe. "I mean, he really seems to be quite a down-to-earth kinda guy, but you couldn't have known that from the beginning." Holly took the fireplace lighter from the drawer in the little antique curio shelf over the mantle and lit a yellow scented candle on the coffee table between the couches.

The aroma of citrus began to permeate the air as she replaced the lighter and answered, "Well, to tell you the truth, I *was* a little awestruck but just briefly because that's when the plane started to bounce around a little." Since that story had been recounted on the trip home from the airport the night before, she moved on to more important aspects of the trip and told them about how Chris had seemed preoccupied at certain times and unhappy at other times and about how she had felt such an urgent need to pray for him from time to time. She also told about their time in the park and how Chris had really seemed tense that day. She was grateful for Stephen's sensitivity to the Holy Spirit's nudge to invite Chris to accompany him on a walk now...she believed the timing was right, and talking with a man would give him perspective. Especially when she was sure Stephen would tell him stories of how his life hadn't been perfect either.

Just then the back door opened and Stephen and Chris came in. "Boy, it's hot!" Chris exclaimed as he fluttered his t-shirt back and forth from his chest several times.

"Well, you know the old cliche, 'It's not the heat, it's the humidity!'" Stephen added as they walked into the family room. "Ready for me to fire up the grill?" he asked as he turned to Holly.

"Yeah, the meats are in the fridge. We'll get everything else ready." She turned to Keith and asked, "Would you get something and wipe down the deck chairs and table and raise the umbrella?"

"Sure thing," he replied as he strode to the laundry room for an old rag.

The next couple of hours or so of the evening were taken with preparing and eating the meal, which included discussions on a wide range of subjects, all of which everyone participated in and enjoyed very much. Afterwards, everyone pitched in and helped clean up then went back outside to sit on the deck. The air had begun to cool down as they sat for the next couple of hours talking about anything and everything, and the sky was clear as dusk settled and the stars began to come out. Although the mosquitoes were not out in full force yet, Stephen asked Michael to light the tiki torches anyway just for the light. Everyone sat quietly, enjoying the flickering light and taking in the magnificent celestial view.

After awhile Chris said quietly, "I haven't been this still in a long time." He continued his gaze at the sky as he said, "I wonder how long it took God to create each star and place it in its spot in the sky."

Stephen saw this as an open door and stepped through, saying, "It probably didn't take Him long...and isn't it amazing that the same God that created the universe created us and cares about us in every way? Whatever is important to us is important to Him, no matter how small a thing we think it is."

Chris gave Stephen a knowing look as he said, "Yeah, I'm beginning to understand that." He looked around at the others and could see them all smiling and looking at him.

"I had hoped someday you would," Holly said softly.

Chris said, "You know, you folks are not what I have in mind when I think of Christians."

"Oh, yeah?" Keith asked.

"Nah," Chris answered, leaning up and resting his elbows on his knees and looking down.

"What do you think of when you think of Christians?" asked Holly with a grin. Chris looked up at her then back up at the sky as he leaned back against his chair.

"Well," he began. "I think of stern faces and Bible thumpers and people saying what you can do and what you can't do and thinking that you have to be at church all the time. I guess I'm talking about people I knew growing up. They didn't seem to have much fun either, like you have to give up having a good time if you become a Christian."

"Hmm," Michael hummed. "What makes you think that?"

"Well," Chris began. "I guess that's just sorta how it was when I was growing up. See, my grandfather was a fire-and-brimstone preacher, and when I was living with his relatives, we went to his church sometimes, really just to pacify him. He would come down on us pretty hard if we didn't show up for several weeks. I figure that's no reason to go to church... just because someone will get on your case if you don't."

"You figure right," Keith interrupted.

Chris continued, "The folks at his church all had these stern faces and looked you up and down if you didn't look or act like they thought you should." He chuckled and said, "My grandfather would give my aunt the business if she let it slip that she had mended a pair of pants on Sunday because that was considered work and you just didn't do ANY kind of work on Sunday where I was raised." He shook his head and looked down.

"Sounds like a church full of Pharisees, loading folks down with *rules* and not lifting a finger to help them with the burden," Michael said, shaking his head. "The only standards you have to live by are God's and the only way you're gonna know what His standards are is to read His Book. A few of those rules will still stand because they're biblical, but you won't find many of them in The Bible because a lot of them are just manmade, for whatever reason."

"And about working on Sunday," Stephen said, "Jesus says the Sabbath was made for man, not man for the Sabbath."

Keith added, "And when you become a Christian, your "want-tos" change. You go to church because you want to, you set time aside for God because you want to, you read The Bible because you want to, you're nice to people because you want to be, get it? You want to do some things differently. It's not always easy to live by, but your want-tos really do change."

Rose said, "And it doesn't mean all your problems will go away. Sometimes you'll lose some problems and acquire others; sometimes things get better and sometimes things just change, but you won't get any of us here to say that we'd go back to living without Jesus. You might not lose all your problems, but you'll at least have a way to handle them... Jesus is the Way."

Chris looked thoughtful for a minute, then they all noticed that the wind began to blow softly. "Looks like a storm may be blowing in," Stephen said, looking up at the clouds. The stars were gradually disappearing behind them.

"Yeah, I noticed about a hour ago that it's getting a little muggy and warm. Odd since it had started to sorta cool down just after we ate," Holly added.

"We don't have to go in yet, do we?" asked Chris. It was a rare privilege for him to sit outside under the stars. Also, he was intrigued by this sudden change in the weather.

"Oh, no, no. Not until the lightning starts," Holly answered. "I like a good storm."

They sat and talked another half hour or so then Holly said, "Does anyone notice that the air is getting still?"

Keith said, "Yeah, you're right." Just then they noticed in the distance a small streak of lightning and a few seconds later a faraway clap of thunder.

They sat for a few more minutes then the lightning and thunder began to grow closer and closer until they decided they'd better go in. "I don't like the stillness I feel," Holly said, surveying the night sky as she stood and turned her chair facing against the side of the house. She had been in a tornado several years earlier and had learned to read the signs in the storms. She turned to Chris and said, "South Georgia is prone to electrical storms, especially this time of year because the seasons are changing and the air is becoming unstable. Normally they don't do much harm, but sometimes they turn into tornadoes."

"You should know, Mom," Rose said with a knowing look as she let the deck umbrella down.

"What do you mean?" Chris asked wide eyed as he and Stephen slid the wrought iron table next to the house.

"Well," Stephen said as he put his chair in place beside Holly's. "Holly was in a tornado a few years back. Scared the stew out of her."

"Yeah, but God healed me from being afraid of storms. Haven't been scared since. Go figure," Holly laughed as she helped Stephen tie the table and chairs to the hooks Stephen had installed after a storm had mangled a new deck set several years ago.

"Is that how He handles things sometimes?" Chris asked frowning.

"Yeah. Sometimes He takes you around the storm, but sometimes he takes you through the storm and you become a stronger person, a stronger Christian, because of it," Michael answered, turning the remaining chairs toward the house and tying them to the others.

"You wanna put out those torches, Chris?" Stephen asked as he entered the house.

"Sure," Chris said as he started for the edge of the deck. Just then a bolt of lightning hit a tree in the neighbors' yard.

"Yikes! Hurry, guys!" Holly yelled running for the door. "It's coming up fast!"

"You don't have to tell *me* twice!" Chris answered, extinguishing the last tiki torch and following closely behind her.

After they were all inside and Stephen had secured the door, he said, "Let's round up the flashlights, radio, and batteries. I'll get my police radio and duty bag. Michael, would you get the matches from the cabinet? Keith and Rose, find a couple of candles and we'll be all set."

"Police radio?" Chris asked Rose, as she passed him to get the candles.

"Yeah, Daddy is a volunteer police officer. They'll probably call him out for duty if this thing kicks up like I think it will."

"Cool!" Chris exclaimed.

"You boys want to come along if I'm called out?" Stephen asked the three guys. "I know Rose and Holly would rather stay here."

Rose and Holly laughed as Rose said, "Ya think?"

"I'd like to go!" Chris exclaimed, always up for an adventure.

"Okay, then get ready to work," Michael said.

"Sure. What'll I have to do?" Chris asked.

"Oh, just get rained on and windblown jumping in and out of the car helping move trees and limbs out of the streets," Keith answered nonchalantly.

"The possibility exists that you might have to lend a hand with injured people, too, but let's hope not," Stephen added.

"I'm ready!" Chris answered.

"Do you have a jacket that you don't mind getting wet?" Stephen asked him.

"Not really. I only brought one light jacket," he answered with a perturbed look.

"That's okay. You and I are about the same size, 5'11", size medium, right? Let's see if we can find you one of mine," Keith assured him as he motioned for Chris to follow him to his room. "I think I have an extra one that's water repellant." In the meantime, Stephen's duty bag had been placed by the back door, and the flashlights, radio, candles, matches, and police radio had been set on the coffee table in the family room. The family had taken seats to watch the weather reports on television. Keith and Chris joined them and they all settled in to wait for a call for Stephen's help.

CHAPTER ELEVEN

They didn't have to wait long. Within minutes the phone rang. "Hello? Sure. Where do you need me?" Stephen asked Police Chief Thornton. "Yeah...Okay... Sure... Okay,'bye." He turned to the others and, picking up his jacket and duty bag, said, "There are trees falling on the west side of the county as we speak. Chief says it's looking like it's coming this way in a hurry..." He looked toward the TV. "And it appears he's right." At that everyone turned toward the TV just as an emergency warning scrolled across the screen, naming their county as one in the path of a tornado! The local weather anchor appeared and showed on the map the bright red cell carrying the twister. "This one's a bad one, folks," he began, and continued the usual warning to people in that area that they should take cover.

Everyone looked at each other and for a few seconds no one said a word. Then Stephen broke the silence with, "Chris, are you sure you want to do this? The three of us have all had differing levels of training."

Chris looked from one guy to the other and said, "Unless you think I'll be in the way, I'd really like to help." The previous excitement in his voice had been replaced with sincerity and earnest.

"Well, it'll be dark and things will be happening so fast that I don't think you'll be recognized, and you will most assuredly not be in the way...we'll need every hand we can get," was Stephen's welcome reply. He had an instinct about these things, and that, coupled with the weather anchor's words, caused him to think it was indeed going to be worse than they thought. Rose went for more flashlights for the men while Holly packed bottles of water in a small cooler and crackers and candy bars in a bag. Holly was a stickler for being prepared and always kept supplies on hand for Stephen to take on incidents so that he could keep up his strength as he served the community. Sometimes it was hours before he could get a break. She was glad that she had recently replenished the supply. There was enough for all four to have plenty for the night.

"Let's pray," said Holly as she stretched her hands out to take the hands of Rose and Stephen. Each took another's hand as the solemn group formed a circle in the middle of the family room. "Father," Holly began, "please protect these men as they go out into the night to help with this storm. Watch over and protect them and give them wisdom to know what to do and courage to do it. Let them be the witnesses You call them to be. Bring them back to us safely and protect everyone else out there tonight. Be glorified in it all. In Jesus' Name," she held off on "Amen," giving someone else the chance to add to the prayer.

"And please protect Rose and Holly while we're away," added Stephen.

There was a lull and when no one else had anything to add, Stephen ended it with, "In Jesus' Name, Amen." Chris felt very small and insignificant. He knew he couldn't be "the witness" that Holly had prayed they would be. She knew it, too, but she knew that he needed to hear the prayer for the other men. Maybe he would see what it means to be a Christian witness by watching Stephen, Keith, and Michael live it out before him. Holly held hope that tonight Chris would come closer to a definite decision for the Lord.

There were hugs all around, and the men put on their jackets and headed for the back door, Stephen grabbing his duty bag as he started out. He and Michael turned and kissed their wives as Chris and Keith got into Stephen's car. "Be careful, Baby," Holly said to Stephen as he turned toward the car.

"You, too," Rose said to Michael.

"We will," they promised. Michael suggested to Rose that she stay the night with her mom, and she quickly agreed to do so.

Chris watched the scene as he took his seat in the back of the SUV and wished he had that kind of love in his life... not just the love of a wife but the love of a family. He was someone they really didn't know, yet they were accepting him and loving him anyway. He wished the kind of love they were showing him was something permanent in his life. It had begun to be a deep desire. He had to have that... somehow.

As Stephen drove the car away into the night, they all smiled and waved. Rose and Holly went back into the family room and sat down in front of the TV. There would be no going to bed any time soon for either of them...there was too much tension with regard to the unknown. How long would the storm last? How much damage would the tornado do? Would anyone be injured? Or worse? Each knew the other was concerned for the men, but neither said so. They silently watched as the weather anchor pointed out the red cell and repeated his cautions. As they realized it was coming their way, Rose said, "Don't you think it would be a good idea to go ahead and put our things in the bedroom in the basement?"

"Yeah, let's do that. Then we can watch the weather bulletins until we need to go down. There are snacks and bottles of water already down there, but I'll pack a cooler with ice so we can chill the water. There are pillows and blankets in plastic bags in the closet down there, too, and there are a couple of extra cell phone batteries in that drawer," Holly said as she pointed to the kitchen junk drawer and retrieved the cooler from a cabinet. "Let's take our purses down, too. If the house is hit, we don't want our credit cards blown to the next state!" Holly laughed nervously as she thought of another reason for having their purses nearby. Purses contain driver's licenses and driver's licenses could be used for identification purposes, should that be necessary. Rose glanced back at the TV as she closed the drawer. The red cell was growing larger and moving in their direction.

"Mom, it's time to go, don't you think?"

Holly looked at the TV and said, "Well, from past experience, yeah, I think you're right." This was the second time Holly had headed for their basement in a storm, the first being a false alarm, but, nevertheless, she had been grateful for the basement. She had been alone and it had made her feel safe that day. The other tornado she had experienced was in north Georgia and she had been with her mother-in-law. It had been small but no less frightening. They had escaped unharmed. However, the same could not be said for the minivan she'd driven at the time. They never knew what had struck it because whatever it was had hit and run, but it had pretty much demolished the vehicle. They had always assumed it was a tree since her mother-in-law's previously tree-filled yard had become a virtual desert that night.

They picked up their flashlights, and Holly got the battery-operated radio and extra batteries. As they took their load down the steps, Rose said, "Sounds like the wind is picking up."

"Uh-huh," was Holly's only answer. She knew that sound all too well.

"I'll cover the window," Rose said as she threw everything in a large chair.

"Let me help you," Holly said as she strode to the window. Keith was a drummer in a Christian rock band in its formative stages but also ran a recording studio out of their basement as a sideline, so his chairs came in handy. After the false alarm, Stephen had installed brackets at the top and bottom of the window and cut a piece of thick plywood a little bigger than the window so that in the event that they should need the basement again for a storm, the wood could simply be lifted onto the brackets to cover the window. Flying glass could prove deadly if the window were shattered during a tornado. It was only a half basement, but it was finished and had a small windowless bedroom and bathroom to one side, so they would hole up there to ride out the storm and, if necessary, they could sleep there.

The wind began whipping and growing louder, and the thunder and lightning grew brighter, louder, and more frequent. Holly had adjusted the radio to the local station and she and Rose listened as the weather bulletins also became more frequent. Then the radio went silent. Apparently, the station's tower had been hit. A few seconds later the electricity went out.

"Should we turn on the flashlights yet?" Rose asked her mother as they took each other's hands.

"Let's hold off until we have to," Holly answered. They sat in silence for just a few minutes when all of a sudden she said, "Turn on your flashlight and get your things." As they picked up their pillows and blankets, Holly exclaimed loudly, "Let's go! Let's go!" and pushed Rose toward the bedroom. They ran in and slammed the door just as they heard the window shatter and the plywood splinter into pieces.

"Turn off your flashlight!" Holly exclaimed as she turned hers off. As they heard the sound of trees snapping, the wind howling, the thunder booming, and things falling in the other side of the basement and saw the flashes of lightning under the door, each woman prayed silently, not only for their protection and the protection of the house but for the men and for their whole community. As quickly as the wind had come upon them, it died down, and everything was silent except for an occasional thunder clap. The women could hear each other breathing heavily and their own hearts pounding in their chests.

"It's over," Holly breathed, her voice shaking. In just a moment her cell phone rang, then Rose's. They each turned on their flashlight and answered with a shaky, "Hello?" After telling their husbands that they were okay, hearing them relay the good news to Keith and Chris, and their collective sigh, the men wanted to know what the condition of the house was.

"We haven't even had a chance to go out of the bedroom and check," Holly said as she turned her flashlight toward the door. As they went through it, their lights fell on broken glass and splintered wood, overturned chairs and recording equipment, all covered in water from the spray that came through the window as it broke. Thankfully, it had happened so quickly that there was not much water to clean up from the floor. "Well," Holly began, "it's not the prettiest sight I've ever seen, and not nearly as bad as it sounded, but it certainly could have been a lot worse."

She described the scene, and Stephen said, "Thank you, Lord." He sighed then asked, "Can you get to the steps so you can go upstairs and check on the house?" Holly shined her flashlight in the direction of the steps and found that they were wet but clear. "Yes," she answered. "Give me a minute to climb them...my legs are jelly."

Stephen laughed and said, "Understandable. Take your time." Rose followed her up, and at the top of the stairs they separated so that they could assess the damage more quickly.

"It doesn't seem that anything is disturbed on the east end," Holly said as she shined her light over each room on the kitchen end of the house. "How about it, Rose?" she called down the hall.

"Everything looks okay," she called back from the west end. "Praise...the...Lord," Stephen said quietly as he breathed a sigh of relief. "I have to tell you, honey, that's a miracle. If you could see the rest of the city, you'd think we were in a war zone! Trees down, power lines down, cars overturned, houses demolished, and I can't even describe the mobile home parks. The Sheriff's Department says the rest of the county was only hit in random spots, but it's pretty bad all over."

"Are there any serious injuries or fatalities?" was Holly's next question.

"Well, unfortunately, there are two fatalities on the west end of the county. I didn't recognize their names or addresses. I've also heard that there are some injuries, but I don't know where or to what extent." Then, "Okay, Chief!"

"Listen, baby, I have to go. Chief Thornton is calling for us. I have no idea when we'll be in, but it'll be awhile. If you need me, just call, okay?"

"I will, but everything looks okay for us here. Don't worry. We'll be fine," Holly assured him.

"Promise you'll call if you need us?"

"I *promise*, honey. Don't worry."

"Okay, I love you. 'Bye"

"I love you, too. 'Bye."

Rose had already hung up and was heading back down the steps when her mother stopped her. They could hear the emergency vehicles now and see their flashing lights as they passed by. Holly said, "Let's look out the windows and try to see what it looks like when the flashing lights go by. Maybe that will shed some light on the situation."

"Oh, Mom! Do you have a joke for every occasion?"

"Almost!," Holly retorted, laughing.

They went into the living room and peered through the windows as the emergency vehicles passed by, slowly assessing the damage. Although it was really too dark to tell, it appeared that the neighbors all around them had lost parts of their roofs and lots of trees, but it appeared that the Monroes had lost only one small tree in the front yard. "What a miracle," Rose whispered in amazement.

Holly stood with her mouth open in awe. After a few minutes of taking in the unbelievable sight, she asked, "Don't suppose we can see in the back yard, do you?" as she turned toward the back of the house. She tried to look through the kitchen window, but all she could see with her small flashlight was debris that had blown onto the deck. She walked through the house checking the ceiling in each room to be sure there was no sign of roof damage. Everything looked clear, so she joined Rose who had stepped out into the garage. "See anything interesting?" she asked as she stood behind her SUV.

"Well," Rose began, "it looks like there's a tree across the driveway, so the guys may have to move one more tree before they can call it a night...whenever that is." They shined their flashlights and looked as best they could, not venturing around the yard for fear of stepping on a live wire.

Holly began to yawn as she announced that she was going inside. Rose followed her mother up the steps and into the kitchen, yawning, too. "Why is it that when one person yawns everyone else in the room joins in?" Rose laughed as she rubbed her eyes.

"I don't know, but your father's the worst. All he has to do is hear the word 'yawn,' and his mouth gapes open!" They laughed, and Holly said, "I think I'll tell the guys about the tree in our driveway."

She called and Stephen answered, puffing, "Yeah? Is there a problem?"

"No, I just wanted to let you know that there's a tree across our driveway, so unless you want to park on the street and walk to the house in the rain, you boys will need to save some energy to move one more tree before you turn in tonight."

"Okay, but I can't tell you when that will be. It's worse than anyone thought."

"Really? How so?" she asked.

"There are more injuries and more damage than anyone first suspected. The south side of town was hit worse than first drive-throughs showed. We rode by Rose and Michael's and everything is okay there, not even a missing shingle."

"Well, that's good news!" Holly said.

"If everything looks okay there, why don't you girls go to bed and get some sleep. You never know what you may be called on to do tomorrow."

"Okay, but I'll have my cell phone by the bed so you can call me if you need anything. How are the snacks holding out?"

"Fine. We still have a few left, and a couple of other wives sent stuff with their husbands. Also, the Red Cross is setting up right now, so don't worry. We'll be taken care of. Okay?"

"Okay."

"Good-night."

"Good-night, love."

"Well, I suppose we need to find something to put over that gaping hole in the basement. No need for more rain and who-knows-what-else to come in," Holly suggested. Rose followed her mother to the basement and helped tape plastic trash bags over the hole ripped by the tornado. "Whoever said that man's best friend is a dog didn't know about duct tape!" Holly laughed as she slapped her last piece of gray tape over the bags.

"Yep, a dog would've never stuck," Rose said without cracking a smile as she smoothed her last piece of tape. Her dry sense of humor had always been entertaining to everyone who knew her.

"Rose, you're a crackup," her mother laughed. "Hopefully, the guys will have time tomorrow to do something with this, even if it's just nailing some plywood over it. We'll also need to sweep up the glass and wood and dry the floor. I knew there was a reason we didn't put carpet down here. I'm just glad there wasn't any more water than this that blew in."

The women went upstairs and decided to turn in, so they straightened up the house and got ready for bed. Rose headed for her old room, which was now the guest room. Seeing Chris's things on the bed reminded her that the room was already taken.

"Why don't you just bunk with me tonight?" Holly asked, putting an arm around Rose.

Rose giggled and said, "That might be fun...reminds me of the little pajama parties we used to have when I was in high school." They headed for Holly and Stephen's room and Holly remembered the many times when she and her daughter had stayed up for hours after Stephen and Keith had gone to bed...sometimes crying, sometimes giggling, sometimes just because they wanted to be together. It had been a long time, and she was sorry that they were both so tired and that tomorrow might require stamina. It would be nice to stay up giggling with her daughter again.

"You know something that really irks me?" Rose asked as she turned down the bed.

"What's that?" Holly answered as she lifted the afghan from the foot of the bed, folded it, and laid it across the chair by the window. Stephen's mother had crocheted it for them as a wedding gift so many years ago. It was sky blue with a thin white stripe lovingly woven through the middle. Cassie had been a dear, sweet lady, full of charm and grace. There was no end to her generosity, not only to her family but also to all those with whom she had come in contact. She was loved and missed by many.

"People asking when Michael and I are going to have a baby. That irks me. We've only been married two years," Rose continued with the slightest pout. She wasn't given to pouting, but she could be riled pretty quickly when certain topics arose. "Don't people realize that's none of their business? What if we don't want children, which we do, but what if we didn't? And what if we can't have children? Don't they realize how awful that would make us feel every time we heard the question?" Holly smiled as she remembered hearing the question so many times. It had taken her and Stephen years to have each of their children, and, yes, the question had cut through her heart so many times. She had learned early on never to ask that question of a couple, no matter how long they had been married.

"I know, honey," she said quietly. "I know, but people sometimes...many times...speak before they think. There's an old saying: 'Some people shoot first and then aim.' People who had their children early and easily just haven't stopped to think how blessed they were. They never had to endure those questions, so it doesn't occur to them that they could be hurtful. They mean no harm."

"Well, I'll never ask anyone that question," Rose retorted as she snuggled down beneath the clean blue sheets.

Holly sat down on Stephen's side of the bed as she rubbed the last of the hand lotion between her fingers. She always slept on that side when he was away. "Gotta put lotion on my grocery list," she said with a yawn as she turned out her flashlight and laid down.

"Mom," Rose's voice was quiet in the still darkness.

"Yeah, honey?"

Rose hesitated then asked, "Were you ever sorry you had us?"

Holly was taken aback at the question. "Rose! What a question! Of course not!" She quickly added, "Were there times when I could have pulled my hair out? Absolutely, but never a time when I wished you weren't here. Yikes! What a question!" Holly gave a soft punch to Rose's arm in the dark.

"Oh, I knew the answer. I just wanted to hear you say it," Rose giggled.

"You silly," Holly said as she turned over. "Good night, honey."

"Good night, Mom. I love you."

"I love you, too, baby girl."

CHAPTER TWELVE

In her exhaustion Holly had forgotten to pull the curtains before going to bed, and the early morning sun was streaming in. She got up to shut them, fully intending to go back to bed, remembering Stephen's caution that today might be a busy one. Stephen was right...he was always right, it seemed...and today would be no different. As she approached the window she gasped in horror. She didn't know what she had expected to see, but this wasn't it.

The Baileys' roof next door was missing some shingles, but across from the Baileys the Austins' roof was gone, and so were the Austins, as evidenced by their empty carport. Obviously they had spent the night elsewhere. Across the street from the Monroe house, there wasn't a tree left standing in the Bakers' yard, front or back, but the house seemed fine. *God, you are awesome. Thank you for sparing them.* The Bakers had just been through some financial problems. Mrs. Baker had needed surgery and the medical bills had stacked up. They were just completing their last payments on them and surely didn't need the added expense of house repairs. She was glad a police car had come by last night and checked on everyone. Stephen had made sure of that.

The neighborhood was small, just the four houses, and they were a close-knit group, very much like a family. The Baileys were a newlywed couple who had only lived in their house for a few months. The Austins were a family of six, so losing their roof was major to them. They would obviously have to stay with nearby family for awhile, which would be an inconvenience to everyone involved. The Bakers were the grandparents of the neighborhood family, having just celebrated their 50th wedding anniversary. Their four children lived out of town, so they had adopted all the younger people of the neighborhood as grandchildren and great-grandchildren, and they were all crazy about their adoptive grandparents. When the Bakers had hit on financial hard times, the little neighborhood had rallied around them with all kinds of support, mainly because of Jack and Sue Baker's godly influence over the years. They had taught by example the scripture that says we're supposed to bear one another's burdens. Any time one of the neighbors was in need, Jack and Sue had been there with whatever they could offer. The Bakers and the Monroes were the only Christians among them and had gathered many times to pray for the salvation of their neighbors, and they believed they would some day see it happen.

Rose had awakened at her mother's gasp and jumped up to see what was going on. She couldn't believe her eyes. The little neighborhood was a mass of trees, limbs, shingles, housing insulation, and other unidentifiable debris. Garbage cans and lawn furniture littered the street. "Didn't Daddy say it looked worse out there than they first expected? If our neighborhood looks like this, then what must the rest of the area look like?"

"I have a bad feeling," Holly said as she turned to her closet and took out jeans and a t-shirt. "I'm going to take a shower. Got a feeling it's going to be a long day."

After starting up the generator so they would have electricity, she headed back upstairs for the bathroom as Rose said, "Want me to make us some breakfast?"

"That'd be great. We're probably going to need a big one today," came Holly's reply as she turned on the shower, grateful they had a well and a gas-powered generator.

As Rose started for the kitchen, her cell phone rang. It was Michael. He sounded tired as he told her that they were returning to the house and were really hungry. "I'm just starting breakfast, so I'll make enough for all of us."

"Mom," she called as she closed her cell phone. "The guys are on their way home."

"Okay, thanks," Holly called back.

A few minutes later Holly could smell bacon cooking and was suddenly famished. She finished her shower, dressed, and just as she was tying her tennis shoes, she heard the back door open and shut and knew the men were back.

She came down the hall and into the family room as she heard Keith say, "Mmmmm, bacon and eggs...I can't wait!"

"And grits and biscuits and jam," Rose added to the menu. "And if you're still hungry, I saw some cinnamon rolls in the freezer and popped them in the oven."

"Mom's homemade cinnamon rolls?!" gasped Keith, brown eyes wide as he turned his questioning gaze to his mother.

"Yep," Holly nodded.

"Oh, man. I love breakfast," said Chris as he straddled the stool at the breakfast bar. "Even the grits!" he grinned.

"Well, my wife makes one of the best breakfasts you'll ever eat. Even the grits," Michael smiled proudly as he put his arm around Rose's shoulders.

"One day I'm gonna have one of those," Chris said smiling.

"A spatula?" Rose teased, holding up the one she was cooking the eggs with.

"No, silly, a wife!" he returned with a sarcastic grin.

"Yeah, me, too," said Keith. "I hope," he added with his own sarcasm. They all laughed as Michael and Keith took the jackets and hung them in the laundry room to dry. They would probably need them later on in the day.

"God has a girl for you. Just wait and see," Holly assured her son as she set the table and Rose placed the steaming platters of food on the island. "Both of you," she added winking at Chris, who only smiled.

She liked to serve large meals buffet style from the island and was glad they had included it in the kitchen plans when they had built their house. Everyone gathered at the table and held hands as Stephen asked the blessing, which included words of thanks to God for sparing their lives and belongings. Then they helped their plates and settled at the table to enjoy the bountiful breakfast. The food refreshed the tired, hungry men.

Just as they were finishing off the last of the cinnamon rolls, Stephen's cell phone rang. "Hey, Chief. What's up?" He listened quietly. When he didn't say anything for a minute, everyone stared at him to see what was going on. "Okay, we'll be there in a few minutes." He looked serious.

"What's wrong, honey?" Holly asked.

"It's Macey."

"What's the matter, Stephen?" Holly asked, a fearful look crossing her face.

"She was on her way home from her business trip when she got caught in the storm. Her car was spotted down an embankment by a truck driver."

Holly's bottom lip started to tremble as tears welled up in her eyes. "Where is she now?"

"Chief said they're loading her into the ambulance right now."

"Let's go," said Holly as she jumped from her chair and ran for her purse and phone.

"I'll take her," Rose volunteered as she jumped from her seat, peeling off Holly's white bathrobe. "You men are tired and I know you all want a shower. I'll throw on some clothes and get her to the hospital. When you're ready, you can follow."

"Rose, be careful. There are power lines down everywhere," her father warned.

"I will, Daddy."

Keith noticed the look on Chris's face and anticipated his question. "Macey is Mom's closest cousin. All our other family lives three hours away in north Georgia. Macey moved here to go to college, got a good job here, and just decided to stay. We moved here years later."

"Oh," Chris nodded, avoiding unnecessary conversation. He knew he'd be brought up to speed later.

Rose was back in a flash, dressed, with purse in hand, and Holly emerged from the bathroom, face red and eyes swollen. "I'll be all right, honey," she said noticing Stephen's concerned look as she kissed him on the way out the door.

"We'll call you," said Rose as they closed the back door behind them.

"Look, guys," began Chris. "This is your family and I know you want to be with them. I don't know Macey. Let me clean up the kitchen while you shower. I'll stay here and rest, then when you guys get back from the hospital, you can rest and I'll do whatever is needed with Rose and Holly."

"Would you? Are you sure?" Stephen gave Chris an appreciative look.

"Of course. Don't think about it again."

"Thanks, man. I owe you," Stephen said as he, Keith, and Michael headed for the showers. Chris smiled and nodded as he started clearing the table.

You'll never owe me anything, Chris thought as he remembered this family's many kindnesses to him and the genuine love they had showed him in the last few days. He was used to yes men, groveling fans, infatuated women, and gold diggers...not real love. He had never felt so loved as he did now. Never.

He finished up the dishes and was sitting on the couch when one by one the men emerged from the three bathrooms still looking tired but at least refreshed from the showers. "Unless you want to shower now, I'm going to turn off the generator to save fuel," said Stephen.

"Go ahead. I know how to turn it on if I need it, Chris replied.

"Okay, be right back," Stephen promised as he trotted down the steps to the basement. He was back in a few seconds. "We'll be back as soon as we can. Make yourself at home. Take a nap. Whatever you want to do. You're at home here," Stephen said as the men headed for the back door. "Chief sounded like Macey's injuries are pretty severe, so I don't know how long we'll be."

"It's all right. Take your time. I probably *will* take that nap," Chris said.

"Okay, see you later," Michael said as they left.

Chris thought about what Stephen said, "Make yourself at home. You're at home here." He was alone for the first time in awhile, and his mind wandered back to his childhood and the homes he'd had. Or rather the houses he had lived in. He couldn't really call them homes. His parents had both been murdered when Chris was three, a case still unsolved, and he had been placed in the custody of his grandparents for a few years. At their deaths in a car accident four years later, he had been pawned off on relative after distant relative, even spending a short time in an unloving foster home until, at the age of 16, he had dropped out of school and struck out on his own.

Living on the road has to be better than this, he had thought. No one had even come looking for him. Life had been hard, and the road had been long and sometimes lonely, sometimes filled with too many of the wrong kinds of people. He knew that now. He had considered himself lucky to have fallen into show business the way he had. He had waited tables in Los Angeles, and a movie producer had noticed his good looks, despite the jagged scar on his forehead, and thought he was worth the risk, so he got him a small part in a movie, and he had worked ever since, never looking back. Chris had always been a rover, but that life was getting old...and boring...and tiring. He was 35 years old now, and the only desire he had ever had besides to have *come* from a loving family was to *create* a loving family, the fulfillment of which had eluded him. He had not trusted any of the women who had hung on him over the years. *They're not for real. They only want to be known as Chris Lapp's wife and to spend Chris Lapp's money,* he had thought, and he was right...and had never married.

He yawned and looked out the window at Holly's flower pots blooming on the deck. One terra cotta pot of pink petunias looked especially familiar to him as he drifted off to sleep.

He awoke at 1:30 to a quiet house and realized he was still alone. Either things were pretty bad at the hospital or Macey was able to talk and her family was just spending time with her. His guess was that the hospital was full, judging from the number of injured people they had encountered the night before. Chris had time to reflect on the scenes of the preceding night. He had never seen so much blood and pain. He had been in movies with that kind of action and scenery, but he had never seen anything like it in real life, and it had affected him. People were more real to him now. That somehow stirred a compassion in him that he had never felt before, and he wasn't sure what to do with it.

Miraculously, the phones were working, either because they never went down in the Monroes' area or they had already been repaired, so he took the cordless phone, just in case someone called, and went outside to walk around the house and look at the gardens again. The air was clean and the sky was clear, a far cry from the scene just hours ago when it seemed the whole world had blown apart. There was something therapeutic about helping people in need, something he had never felt before. No one had ever seemed to need him before, and for the first time in his life he realized that was something that had been missing in his life...the need to be needed. It was unsettling and at the same time comforting. He wasn't sure he could explain that. Most of the people he had assisted the previous night were in shock, either physically or mentally and would never remember him or what had happened, but he would never forget it. It would be many weeks before he could sort out all of his emotions.

Holly's flowers were a mess. The wind and rain and debris had destroyed much of her front beds and almost all of her back beds. *I'm sure she hasn't noticed this yet. She'll be really upset,* Chris thought sadly as he looked around the yard, imagining the look on Holly's face when she would see it for the first time. She so loved her flowers. He was beginning to understand, ever so slightly, the tenderness of heart that it takes to nurture not just flowers but people, too.

His thoughts drifted back to the time in Amsterdam when he sat and watched Holly walking through the tulips and wondering how she could be so happy. Yes, he was beginning to understand just a little bit. The compassion he had felt for those injured people last night was working on him, and it was easier to understand the soft-hearted now. Suddenly he wanted to go see Macey...a woman he'd never seen, a woman he'd never known but somehow felt a compassion for. What was happening to him?

He realized last night, under the cover of darkness and in the midst of rain and wind and chaos, that no one had recognized him; but today, if he tried to go to the hospital and see Macey, his presence would cause a different kind of chaos...

and this was not the time for that. Maybe later he would get the chance to see her.

Without realizing what he was doing, he began picking up branches, large and small, that had fallen out of the trees and into the main flower bed in the back yard. Not knowing where the Monroes usually disposed of yard debris, he made a pile to one side of the yard so that it could be taken care of later. Having finished that job, he decided to try to replant the flowers that had been pulled up by the winds. It seemed to him that digging and placing the flowers and snuggling them down with more dirt was a familiar act, but he had never planted a flower in his life...had he?

Suddenly he realized he was actually helping someone... he was putting feet to the feelings of compassion that had begun to confuse him earlier. There were only a few more plants that needed his help, and he was finished with them in no time. It felt good to know that he had helped Holly avoid more pain.

Just then the Bowdons and Monroes returned from the hospital. Chris walked to the garage as the SUVs parked. "What's the story?" Chris asked anxiously.

"It doesn't look good, Chris," Stephen answered shaking his head as he got out of the vehicle.

"Yeah, Mom won't leave her," Keith said as he got out and walked toward the back door.

"Macey has extensive injuries that will take a long time to heal," Rose added as she picked up her purse, shut her door and headed for the garage to join them. "We prayed and Mom insisted on staying the rest of today and tonight."

"Is Macey conscious?" Chris asked.

"Yes, thankfully she has no head injuries, but they are giving her pain medication that makes her drowsy. Her left arm and both legs are broken and she has some deep cuts on her legs. Her spleen is severely bruised, but the main injury is a very long, deep gash to her back. She lost lots of blood waiting for someone to find her and has no idea how long she waited, so she's weak," Michael answered, stretching his arm.

"Problem?" Rose asked him. "Nah, I just pulled a muscle lifting a tree last night. No biggie." Rose massaged it anyway.

"Yeah, I guess in all the commotion today we haven't found out how things went with you fellas last night," Rose said, setting her purse on the kitchen table and walking into the family room as the others entered the kitchen. "Come in and sit down and tell me what happened."

As they entered, Stephen noticed the lights blinking on the microwave indicating that the clock needed to be reset. "Ah, we have power!"

"Yessss!" Rose cheered.

Stephen also noticed the clean kitchen and said, "I can't thank you enough for cleaning up the kitchen, Chris."

"Forget it. It was the very least I could do after you've shown me such hospitality," Chris said as he strode to the family room and sat down.

"You're a great guy," Stephen said as he dropped into his easy chair, sprawling his legs out in front of him. "One in a million."

Chris tried not to look surprised as he thought, *Is there no end to these people's kindness? A great guy? No one has ever called me a great guy. A good actor, yes, but never a great guy.* He was actually confused but decided to let it pass. Besides, Rose wanted to hear about the adventures of the night before, so they each took turns telling what had happened. Many trees had been moved from roadways and streets and off the tops of cars and houses; bright blue tarps and other plastic coverings had been placed on gaping holes in roofs; many ambulance calls were made and the injured taken to the only hospital in town, which was by now overflowing, and other nearby hospitals were being utilized;

downed wires had been secured so that no one would be hurt; and many other stories were related. The most amazing story of the night to all of them, however, was that only two people had been killed...two too many...but a miracle nonetheless. There were two people taken in with mild heart attacks from all the commotion and fear, but they had been quickly stabilized. There were many others with broken bones and cuts. But Macey's injuries were among the worst.

Chris decided to tell them how he was beginning to feel a compassion he had never known and confided that he wasn't sure where it was coming from and how to deal with it. "God is drawing you, my friend," Stephen said, giving Chris a knowing look and a smile. Keith, who was sitting beside Chris on the sofa, smiled and gave him a soft punch on the bicep, and Michael smiled and threw him a wink. Rose simply smiled and squeezed the pillow she was holding.

I wish Mom were here, she thought.

Chris looked around at them then arose suddenly and declared, "I'm going for a walk." He shot between them and out the back door.

They all looked at each other a little stunned. Then Rose quietly said, "He's scared."

"I know," her father replied. "He'll be all right. God is working on him."

The phone rang and Rose leaned over the sofa to the end table and answered the phone. "Oh, hi, Mom."

"How are things at the house?"

"We're all fine. Everyone seems rested. Chris cleaned up the kitchen while we were gone. Now he's gone out for a walk."

Holly said, "Hmmm, he always takes a walk when something's up. What's the matter?"

Rose laughed. "Funny you should ask. It appears that God is doing something to him...working on him...drawing him. Seems the whole scene last night has left him a little unsure of some newfound feelings of compassion. How's Macey?"

"She's resting. Dr. Allen says that she has a long way to go, but he thinks she's going to be fine, although she'll have a huge scar on her back. Well, I just wanted to check in. I'm gonna go back in her room and try to take a nap. Talk to you later. 'Bye."

"Bye, Mom." Rose filled the guys in on Macey's condition then declared that there were mounds of laundry to do at her house, and she also wanted to check on their neighbors.

"Laundry? Only if the power is on at our house, too," Michael reminded her as he yawned and declared that he needed a nap.

"Oh, shoot! That's right. Well, I still want to check on the neighbors," she answered, so she and Michael left but promised to call regularly for updates.

Keith and Stephen decided while the house was quiet and they weren't expecting Holly to call again for awhile that they would also try to get some sleep. Meanwhile, Chris continued his walk. He had a lot to think about and tried to concentrate and collect his thoughts, but all the damage to the surrounding houses distracted him. How amazing that the people had survived...not only survived but hadn't even been hurt. He wanted to help but at the same time felt so helpless. Then he remembered the Bakers' bills and knew immediately that he would leave money with Holly and Stephen to give to them. He had more than enough for himself and besides he was becoming more well known and would soon be more in demand than ever. He knew that. Lately, his agent and his manager were constantly telling him how popular he was becoming, but for the first time in years it really left him feeling empty and craving whatever it was that would fill that hole.

He stopped in his tracks. Hadn't Holly said something about a God-shaped hole that unsaved people have? Was that his problem? The hole was God-shaped and only God was the perfect fit? That couldn't really be it. Could it? He looked around and took a deep breath. The smell of fresh pine was in the air from all the split and broken trees. One beautiful old magnolia lay in the Bakers' backyard, its blooms still open, white and elegant. Somehow it had missed their swimming pool. He thought of Holly again and how happy the flowers in The Netherlands had made her. The simple things in life seemed to fulfill her.

Funny, he had searched his whole life for happiness and only now realized he had never been happy, not really. He was never happy with any of the families he had lived with, the freedom of being on his own at 16 had not made him happy. Being discovered in the restaurant in Los Angeles had given him a temporary, fleeting happiness of sorts, but making films had begun to grind on him, something he had only recently realized.

He slowly walked back to the Monroe home, turned the knob and went into the kitchen. Thankfully, the guys had left the door unlocked for him. *Ever the thoughtful folks,* Chris thought as he walked quietly to the guest room. The house was quiet as he realized the men were resting, so he closed the door and laid across the bed to think. His eyes grew heavy and the pot of petunias again flashed before his eyes as they closed in restful sleep.

Two hours later he awoke to the sound of chain saws as they buzzed and made firewood of some of the downed hardwoods on the street. He went to the window and saw two men next door at the Bailey house working on an old oak that had fallen across the front porch, making passage through the front door virtually impossible and leaving an enormous gash in the porch floor.

Across the street from the Baileys' he saw a van pull into the driveway, and a man and woman and several children got out. Chris assumed it was the Austins coming back to survey the damage to their house and belongings. And across the street from the Monroes' he saw what had to be kindly Mrs. Baker carrying a plate of cookies and taking careful steps across the street to offer the workmen a snack.

Tears came to his eyes as he thought about all he had missed in life. Thoughtful little ladies, vans full of children, families...and God. Yes, he now knew he had missed God. He had never really thought about Him much since becoming an actor, but slowing down these last few days, being put in his current position where he saw how the other half lives had forced him to think about things he had shoved way to the back of his mind...things he thought he had put *out* of his mind years ago.

He heard bedroom doors open and footsteps in the hallway. Then he heard Keith's and Stephen's voices in the family room. He ran his fingers through his earlobe-length hair as he looked in the mirror and wiped his eyes. Opening the door he could hear the men in the kitchen. They were getting out the makings for sandwiches as he walked in.

"Want a ham sandwich, Chris?" asked Keith as he held up a knife and a piece of whole-wheat bread.

"Sure," was all he could force from his lips.

"Here, open this bag of chips," Stephen said as he tossed the bag across the table. "We're using our finest china and crystal this time," he added with a hint of sarcasm as he pointed to the paper plates and plastic cups. "If there's not a mess in the kitchen there won't be a mess to clean up in the kitchen," he joked, as he washed the one knife they had used to spread mayonnaise and mustard on the bread. He dried it and put it back in the drawer. They sat down, Stephen asked the blessing, took one bite, and the phone rang.

Keith answered it and said, "Yeah, I'll be right there. Okay. 'Bye." He walked back to the table, picked up his sandwich and said, "That was Colby. He wants me to come over and give him a hand with some stuff that got turned over in their yard. I'll just take my sandwich with me. I shouldn't be long."

"Okay, son. See you later."

"See ya, Chris," Keith said as he walked to the door. Chris just nodded and gave him a slight smile.

When the door had shut behind Keith, Chris said, "Stephen, we need to talk." Stephen looked up from his sandwich, picked up a chip, and said, "Sure, man. What's up?' Stephen had a feeling he knew.

"Holly once said in Amsterdam that everyone has a God-shaped hole in their heart." Stephen grinned.

"Yeah, that's a trusted old saying and one of her favorites," Stephen grinned.

Chris remained serious as he said, "I'm ready to fill mine." Stephen swallowed the last bite of his sandwich and drank long from his cup.

"You're serious?"

"As a heart attack." Which he considered more serious than he ever had before.

"You realize you're never going to be the same again?"

"I certainly hope I'm not. There's got to be a better life than the one I'm living now."

"Okay, son." Chris's heart melted.

Son? he thought. *Had anyone ever called him 'son'?* It was the first fatherly thing Stephen had said or done to Chris...and he liked it.

Stephen got up from the table and said, "Come into the family room." He picked up his Bible from the coffee table as he motioned for Chris to sit on the sofa. He then proceeded to tell Chris all the things Holly had said in Amsterdam, being careful to show him scripture at each point. Chris noticed it was the same scriptures that Holly had given him by e-mail in Amsterdam. *John 3:16, "For God so loved the world that he gave his only begotten son that whoever believes in him should not perish but have everlasting life." John 14:6,*

"Jesus said to him, 'I am the way, the truth, and the life. No one comes to the Father except through me." Romans 3:23, "for all have sinned and fall short of the glory of God." Acts 26:18 "to open their eyes in order to turn them from darkness to light, and from the power of Satan to God, that they may receive forgiveness of sins and an inheritance among those who are sanctified by faith in Me." Romans 5:12, "Therefore, just as through one man sin entered the world, and death through sin, and thus death spread to all men, because all sinned." Romans 6:23, "For the wages of sin is death, but the gift of God is eternal life in Christ Jesus our Lord." Romans 5:8, "But God demonstrates his own love toward us in that while we were still sinners, Christ died for us." Ephesians 2:8-9, "For by grace you have been saved through faith and that not of yourselves, it is the gift of God, not of works, lest anyone should boast." John 1:12-13, "But as many as received him, to them he gave the right to become children of God, to those who believe in his name: who were born not of blood, nor of the will of the flesh, nor of the will of man, but of God." I John 5:12, "He who has the Son has life; he who does not have the Son of God does not have life."

Stephen explained what it all meant then asked, "Do you understand all this?"

"Yes, I think I finally get it," Chris answered.

"Is this what you want? You want to confess all your sins to God, realizing that only Jesus can wipe your slate clean, and pray to receive Jesus Christ into your life? You're ready to give your whole life to Him?"

"I can't believe I'm saying this, but yes...I am."

"Okay, let's pray. Do you want to pray or do you want me to lead you in a prayer that you can repeat?"

"I don't know what to say. Just let me repeat what you say."

"That'll be fine. God will know your heart." Stephen bowed his head, and Chris said, "Wait. I want to kneel." Stephen smiled at Chris's act of full surrender to God. They knelt together in front of the fireplace at the end of the coffee table and Chris repeated the words, truly from his heart, and became a new man. A new creature. Instantly.

They got up and Stephen hugged Chris tightly and quoted from 2 Corinthians 5:17, "Therefore, if anyone is in Christ, he is a new creation; old things have passed away; behold, all things have become new." Chris smiled. "I'm your spiritual father now. You gonna be able to live with that?" Stephen teased.

"I'm more than happy living with that, Stephen," was Chris' choked answer as the tears poured down his cheeks and onto Stephen's shirt. He would never be the same again. Praise God, he would never be the same again.

CHAPTER THIRTEEN

The remainder of the afternoon and early evening were uneventful. Good thing because Chris had a lot to think about, and he and Stephen had a long talk about what was on Chris's mind. "Stephen, I feel like a new man! All that guilt is gone! It's like my chest feels lighter!"

Stephen laughed and said, "You ARE a new man, Chris. Remember? 'A new creation?'"

"Oh, yeah! I forgot already!" Chris hit his forehead with his hand.

"That's okay, Chris. God doesn't expect you to remember everything immediately, and He doesn't expect you to grasp everything all at once." He explained to Chris that life was going to be different for him, not that all his problems would go away necessarily–in fact, some would probably go away but others may take their place–but life was going to be different, a "good" different. He told him that he would need to seek out Christian friends when he went home, that God may call him to something other than acting or He might leave him there. Chris realized that Stephen was saying a lot of things that Holly had already told him, which was good. As an actor, Chris knew that repetition is a good mnemonic.

One can never tell what God is going to do. He explained that Chris would need to spend lots of time in prayer and Bible study seeking the leading and guidance of the Holy Spirit because these are the things that keep one in touch with God, that keep one close to God, that keep one from straying. He asked Chris if he knew any Christians that he could spend time with back in California, maybe some people who could include him in their Bible study groups or that he could attend church with. Chris didn't know of anyone that fit that bill, but he was sure he could contact some actors that he knew were Christians but he had never met. Funny, but until now he had never wanted to meet them. He laughed out loud at the thought. His agent, Lorne, would help him contact them. Of course, he would have to explain to Lorne what had happened. He wasn't sure how to do that. All he knew was that he had to. And there would be lots of other people who would need to be told. *Maybe I can even win some over,* he thought as he considered the people he would be meeting with in the weeks to come.

The idea of acting again wasn't particularly exciting now as he thought of all the movies and TV shows he had appeared or starred in and all the sordid parts he had played and all the things he had done that had grieved God's heart. A career rife with raunch. He knew he couldn't return to that. That life was over for him. And he didn't even seem to mind it. Was he strong enough to turn down those offers now, though? He knew he had to, but he surely did dread it. The mocking and ridicule and rejection would be hard to endure. He had signed on to do another movie, one with lots of sordid details, and the shooting was to begin in roughly a month. He had absolutely no desire whatsoever to make that movie. What was he going to do? He discussed it with Stephen and together they decided that he had to contact his lawyer and try to get out of it.

"I've never attempted that before. I never had a reason to. I always wanted to do it all, so whatever came along, I agreed to do. No reason not to. They paid me to act, so I acted."

Stephen said, "Well, you know, just because you become a Christian doesn't mean you automatically have to give up acting. There are lots of Christian actors. They're not among the big box office stars because they refuse to compromise their beliefs and take on the seedy parts, but they're focusing on getting God's message out to the masses. There may not be as much money in Christian films, but the dividends are much greater, don't you think?" Chris thought a minute then decided he liked the idea of bringing what he was feeling now to other people.

"Why don't you concentrate on tying up loose ends right now, contacting those Christian actors, and asking them to hook you up with folks in the Christian film industry?" Stephen suggested.

"Sounds like a plan," Chris agreed. He was beginning to get excited about his future. "Minutes ago I was wondering what I was going to do," Chris laughed, "and now there's a plan."

"God has always had a plan for your life, and here's your opportunity to pray about it...your first opportunity to pray as a Christian. See what God wants you to do. Asking God is always the right thing to do. Just because another Christian suggests something to you doesn't mean it's what God wants. Always go to Him first," Stephen cautioned.

Chris's eyes brightened. "My first prayer since becoming a Christian! Cool! I like it!" Then his shoulders dropped a little as he said with a confused look on his face, "What do I say?"

Stephen laughed as he said, "Just talk to Him. Just say what's on your mind." Chris looked thoughtful. "Want to pray out loud with me here or you want to try it when you're alone?" Stephen asked.

"I want to try it with you here...Daaaad! You're the one who said you're my spiritual father," Chris chided in answer to Stephen's look of confusion.

Stephen laughed. "Okay, go ahead."

Chris and Stephen bowed their heads as Chris began, "God, this is a new day, and I'm not sure what I'm doing, but I'm trusting You to be my Father, so please tell me what to do with my life. Should I stay in acting and try to use it somehow for You, or do You have another direction You want to take me? Please let me know so I won't do something to displease You. In Jesus' Name. Amen." He looked up at Stephen for approval that what he'd said was right and good.

Stephen nodded. "Now keep praying and wait for Him to answer. The answer may come today, tomorrow, next week, or next month, but I'm thinking you won't have to wait long. The answer could come through something you read in the Bible, through talking with other Christians, through circumstances or some other way. God is limitless in how He works."

The pinks and blues and oranges of dusk were appearing through the windows, and Stephen realized they had been so engrossed in their discussion that they had forgotten to eat. "Hungry?" he asked Chris.

"I'm so excited I couldn't eat a bite," Chris answered. "And that's saying something. I'm usually ready to eat any time, night or day!"

Stephen laughed. "That's understandable. I think I'll see if there are any leftovers in the fridge. I'm a little hungry."

"Stephen," Chris began.

"Yeah?" Stephen was bent over peering into the fridge inspecting the containers of leftovers, wondering how long they'd been there.

"Is it possible that compassion comes with becoming a Christian?"

"Sure," Stephen answered without looking up. "Ah, pizza." He shut the refrigerator door and put two pieces of pizza on a paper plate and set it in the microwave. As he pushed the start button he turned his attention back to Chris. Noticing an odd look on Chris's face, he said, "Compassion? For what or whom?"

Chris scratched the back of his head and said, "Well, I know this is going to sound odd, but I've never met Macey and I have this real hurt for her." He gazed at Stephen with a questioning look.

"You, my friend, have just received a new heart. Also..." The microwave beeped and he turned to retrieve his supper. "...when a person becomes a Christian, he receives one or more spiritual gifts. Those are explained in Romans and Corinthians. It will do you good to read up on those. We'll look at those together later, but right now I'll write them down and you can read them by yourself sometime so you can think about what it means to you. I'm suspecting, though, that if you're feeling this compassion strongly right now, you may have the gift of mercy. Just a thought."

Stephen picked up the pen and pad on the island and wrote. Chris was shocked and it showed on his face. "What?" Stephen asked as he took at bite of pizza.

Chris said, "Just doesn't sound like me, that's all."

"You mean it doesn't sound like the *old* you," Stephen said with his mouth full. "Remember? New creation?"

Chris smiled and said, "I think I'm gonna like this new creation thing."

"I think you are, too," Stephen answered with a smile as he reached for a napkin to wipe the pizza sauce dripping onto his chin. "And so will everyone else."

"I want to pray for Macey," Chris said quietly.

"You do?" Stephen asked surprised.

"Yeah. Why the shock?" Chris asked with a grin.

"Boy, when you do something, you jump in with both feet, don't you?"

"What?" Chris asked.

"You just got saved and you're already all into it." Chris frowned in puzzlement.

"That's a good thing," Stephen assured him. "You might want to pace yourself, though." They both laughed and Stephen said, "Okay. Go ahead. Pray for Macey. The practice won't hurt you a bit, and you may be surprised at what'll happen. It's certainly not gonna hurt her."

They bowed their heads as Stephen finished off the last bite of his pizza. Chris began, "God, I don't know Macey, but I feel like You're telling me You want me to pray for her, so here I am. I'm not sure what to say except that these people love her and I love these people. And if they love her, so do I. They're hurting because Macey has been injured, and if they're hurting, I am, too, and I'm asking You to make her well. And whatever You want to do with this compassion thing You've given me, well, just do it. Thank You. In Jesus' Name. Amen."

They looked up and Stephen said, "You're getting good at this. Man, you're taking off like a wildfire!" Chris looked down and grinned. "I wish there were some way I could see Macey, but I don't want to show up at the hospital. You know...the whole celebrity thing." He looked disgusted.

Just then the phone rang. Stephen answered. "Hi, honey." There was a long silence on Stephen's end, but Chris could hear Holly's excited words falling all over themselves as they tumbled out of her mouth. First Stephen's eyebrows went down, then they went up, then he said, "You're kidding!" Chris looked anxiously at him as he waited to hear the news. "Okay, we'll wait up for you. Okay. 'Bye." Stephen hung up the receiver and sat still with his mouth hanging open. "Why am I always shocked when I hear that God has performed another miracle?" he said.

"What? What?" Chris urged, sitting on the edge of a kitchen chair.

"Holly said that Macey's doctor just left. He just examined her wounds and said that they all are progressing in their healing at an unheard-of rate. He said it's like they're ten days ahead of what they should be and that if all goes well with her through the night, he's going to let her go home from the hospital!"

"What?!" was all Chris could say.

"Yeah. He said he looked at her latest blood work and it's like she never lost any blood!" Chris couldn't say anything but just stared with his mouth open. "Chris, do you realize what just happened?" Stephen asked in a little lower voice. Chris just shook his head. "God answered your prayer, man."

"But so fast?" Chris asked in awe.

"God knows what we're going to pray before we pray it, and sometimes He just honors it on the spot like that. He wanted to give you a gift, Chris. I guess you could say it's a 'Welcome home, son' gift." Chris was quiet, then a tear trickled down his cheek. "He loves you so much, Chris," Stephen said.

"I'm beginning to see that a little bit," Chris said as he nodded slowly.

"Ever hear the story of the prodigal son, Chris?"

"Yeah, I think I remember my grandfather preaching about that once or twice. I never paid it any attention, though."

"I'll write that one down, too, and you can look it up and read it."

"Stephen," Chris said sheepishly. "I don't have a Bible. Can I borrow yours?"

"Sure," Stephen said as he walked to the book shelf and took one down. "Here's one you can use till you can get one." But Stephen's gears were already turning. *Note to self,* Stephen thought. *Get Chris a Bible.*

"Guess you'll have a lot to tell Holly when she gets home," Stephen said with a sly smile and a yawn.

Chris laughed and said, "Yeah, I guess I will at that."

Just then the back door opened and Keith came in dragging his feet and yawning. "Well, I was just beginning to wonder where you were!" Stephen said, leaning back in his chair. He and Chris had just taken their conversation into the family room.

"I finished helping with the storm damage and several of us went over to Audrey's."

"Audrey? Who is *that*?" asked Chris raising his eyebrows up and down.

"Wise guy. Audrey's is a *restaurant*...one of only a couple in town not affected by the storm," Keith answered with a punch to Chris's arm. "Somehow they still have electricity." He added nonchalantly, "I did meet a girl today, though. Sarah McMill."

"Oh, really," Stephen questioned. "You like her?"

"Well, I just met her today, but I'll let you know. I'm going to take a shower," he announced as he headed down the hall.

"Peeyew. Please do!" Chris yelled after him with a laugh.

"You're really a wise guy tonight, aren't you? And a poet, too," Keith yelled back.

"It's euphoria!" Stephen yelled after him.

"Your what?" Keith yelled back.

"Never mind. I'll explain after your shower."

"Gimme a break! I know what euphoria is!"

"Yeah, but you don't know why he's all 'euphorized!'"

"Peeyew again," Chris moaned.

"A girl...hmmm. Interesting. Want something to drink?" Stephen asked Chris as he went to the kitchen.

"Just water, thanks," Chris answered. Stephen filled two glasses with ice and water and sat back down, handing one to Chris.

"...out of his belly shall flow rivers of living water," Stephen quoted as he began to drink his down. Chris's eyes widened and he didn't blink as he held his glass in midair. Stephen finished the glass without stopping and, looking at Chris, burst into laughter. "I guess if you've never heard that verse it *would* sound a little strange."

"Ya think?" Chris asked sarcastically, finally taking a drink from his glass. "You *are* going to explain?" he asked as he took another drink.

"Yeah. Okay. Well, it's like this. John 7:38, King James Version, says..." Stephen began.

Keith entered the family room rubbing his straight, brown, wet hair with a towel.

"Quick shower," Stephen said.

He shrugged and said, "Hey, you threw me a carrot. I was curious." Then he plopped down on the couch beside Chris and propped his feet on the coffee table. "Okay. Euphoria," he said looking at his father expectantly.

Stephen turned to Chris, "Remind me later...belly, living water."

Keith looked at Chris then did a double take.

"What?" asked Chris.

"I don't know. You look different somehow," was all he could say. Chris and Stephen looked at each other knowingly.

All of a sudden the back door burst open and Holly came running in. "I could run the mile in 2.2!" she exclaimed, dropping her purse on the kitchen table, throwing her arms up in the air, and kicking the door shut with her heel. Keith gave his dad a puzzled look.

"Dad, she's scaring me again," his feigned look of terror fading into a smile. Stephen said, "I believe your mother has some news," as he stretched his feet out in front of him and clasped his hands behind his head.

"You didn't tell them?!" she yelled with unbelieving eyes. "I told Chris, but Keith just got home," Stephen explained, picking up his glass and draining the few drops of melted ice into his mouth. "Does this have something to do with 'euphoria?'" Keith asked looking from Stephen to Chris and back.

"Huh? Euphoria?" Holly asked puzzled. "Later," Stephen waved her off with his glass. "Go ahead, honey."

"Well, about an hour ago the doctor came into Macey's room with a really confused look on his face, flipping the papers back and forth in her chart. It scared us a little. Well, it scared me more than Macey. You know what a rock she is. Anyway, Macey and I looked at each other and braced for whatever it was that he was going to say. Then he scratched his head, dropped her file on the night stand, flopped down in the chair next to her bed and said, 'We don't know what's happened, but your latest blood work says you never lost any blood.' I asked him what he meant and he said that her blood should not have built up so quickly, even with the transfusions she received. He says all her levels have stabilized in record time."

"Uh-uh. You're kidding!" Keith said in disbelief.

"No, I'm not, and that's not all. Then he checked her wounds, and they had all healed at such a rapid rate that he says it's like she's ten days into the healing process, and if she has a good night tonight she can go home!"

"But they had said it might be weeks before she could go home!" Keith exclaimed.

"I'm beside myself, and you should see Macey. She's ecstatic! She knew she was feeling better and was really surprised that she was, given her injuries and what all the doctor had said at first, but neither of us expected that kind of news." She grew quiet and looked thoughtful for a moment then said, "Why is it that when we get what we pray for we're always surprised?" Chris looked at Stephen and Stephen smiled and waved his arm low as if to say, "The floor is yours."

Chris smiled, took a deep breath and said, "Well, that was a segue if I've ever heard one." Keith and Holly looked at each other, wondering what was coming. Keith walked to his mother's side so that he could get a better view of Chris's face. "It seems there's lots of good news today. What is something else you've been praying for lately, Holly?"

"Well-l-l," she began, "I prayed for rain for the flowers and got a torrential downpour, complete with tornado and gusts to 100 miles an hour." She thought some more, tapping her lips with her fingers. "I prayed for a sick baby in the hospital, and he came back around the bend. He's doing quite well, by the way," she added matter-of-factly.

"Before that," Chris hinted. She shrugged weakly and began, "I can't think of anyth..." she gasped as her eyes grew wide and her mouth dropped open slightly. She stared at Chris then looked at Stephen for confirmation that what she was hoping for was real. Stephen nodded slowly and smiled.

"Euphoria?" Keith asked his father.

"Euphoria," he confirmed with a satisfied smile.

Holly looked at Chris and a tear came to her eye as she whispered, "I want to hear you say it."

Chris knew what was about to happen, and in a shaky voice, with lips quivering, he announced softly, "Holly, today I became a Christian."

She burst into tears as she ran at him and flung her arms around him, almost knocking him down. "I can't believe it!" Tears streamed down Stephen's and Keith's cheeks as they watched Holly and Chris rock back and forth, sobbing. No one could say a word. Just as well...none were necessary.

Keith retrieved a box of tissues from the bathroom and they all laughed as they passed it around, each drawing the white fluff out and cleaning their faces up. They all sat down and the rest of the evening was spent listening to Chris and Stephen tell what had transpired over the past few hours.

"What time did you pray for Macey?" Holly asked curiously.

"Oh, I'd say around nine-ish," Chris answered. "Why?"

Holly smiled and said, "Macey's doctor came in at 9:15."

"Told ya," Stephen said to Chris with a wink.

"Told him what?" Keith asked.

"That sometimes God honors a prayer before it's prayed because He knows what's going to be prayed ahead of time and He just wants to bless our socks off." They spent the rest of the evening just enjoying each other's company and reveling in the memories they knew had been made that day.

When everyone started to yawn, Stephen said, "Well, I guess I'll need to get some sleep. I told the chief I'd be 10-8 with the police department in the morning around 9:00. It's been nice to have this day off and spend it the way I did. God knew all along what was going to happen and that I was needed here more than I was needed out there." He winked at Chris and kissed Holly as he started down the hall to bed. "Good night, all."

"Good night, Dad."

"Good night, honey. I'll be along in a minute."

"Good night, Daaad." Stephen stopped, turned and rolled his eyes at Chris, and chuckled all the way down the hall. Turning to Keith, Chris asked, puzzled, "10 which?"

"10-8 means back in service, back at work with the department."

"Oh, yeah. I should have remembered that," Chris hit himself on the forehead. "I've played a cop, what, three times, now?" Remembering that Holly wasn't home when Keith announced that he'd met a girl, he chided, "Hey, Holly, did you know your son met a girl today?"

"What?" Holly raised her eyebrows. "Do tell."

"Aw, Chris. I just met her today." He turned to his mother. "She's really nice, she's a Christian, and she's lived here all her life. I don't know how I've missed meeting her." Keith scratched his head.

"God's timing," Holly reminded. She had told Keith time and time again that God had someone for Keith and would reveal her to him in His timing.

"Yeah, I know," Keith agreed.

"Do you think you boys could indulge me in the morning?" Holly asked sheepishly.

"How's that?" Chris asked.

"She's having another one of her mushy moments. Just say, 'Yes,'" Keith said shaking his head.

"Yes," Chris obeyed, then leaned to Keith and said, "What did I just agree to?" Keith shrugged his shoulders and looked at Holly.

"I'd just like us all to have breakfast together in the morning. So can I wake you boys up when breakfast is ready?"

"Sure," agreed Chris meekly.

"Hold it!" Keith interrupted. "It depends on when breakfast is being served. If it's 7:00, the answer is a resounding, 'No!' If it's closer to 9:00, maybe."

Holly pulled his ear softly and said, "It most assuredly will NOT be 7:00. I probably won't be up before 8:00. I'm exhausted from this roller coaster ride I've been on the past couple of days!"

"Okay, then, yes, we'll be happy to grace you with our presence at the breakfast table in the a.m." Keith said in his snobbiest voice.

"Great! How does this sound for a menu? Pancakes with warm maple syrup, scrambled eggs with cheese, bacon, biscuits, jelly, honey, coffee, orange juice, and grits, since Chris fell in love with them."

"Sounds great, Mom. Just wake us up." He kissed her on the cheek and went to bed.

Chris remembered he hadn't had supper and said, "I could eat that now! I think I'll have a bite before I go to bed. Is that okay? If I promise to clean up after myself?"

"Sure it is! Unless you want me to cook...'cause that ain't happenin'! I'm going to bed!"

Chris laughed and said, "Oh, no, no! I meant just a sandwich."

"Then go for it."

"Thanks."

Holly looked at Chris and smiled softly as she gave him a hug and said, "God is so good. I'm so happy. Good night, Chris." Then she disappeared down the hall.

Standing there alone in the kitchen he felt so loved, not only by this wonderful family, but by God. A first on both counts. Not only had he never felt the love of a family before, but he had certainly never realized before that God loved him. Even after all the times he had heard the phrase used as a cliche and on sidewalks and in airports over the years from this group and that group, this was the first time he had ever really believed it...and it felt good. He dropped to his knees and rested his hands on his thighs.

"Oh, God," he said as the tears began to stream down both cheeks. "Why do You love me so? Why would You do this for me? Why would you die to save me? Why would You give me these people to love me? I don't understand it all, but I just wanted to tell you, 'Thank You.' I really am grateful to You for all that You are and all that You have done for me already...and I know this is just the beginning. Please don't ever let me disappoint You. I want to live for You that plan that Stephen says You have for me. I have no idea what it is. I just know I want to live it for You. Lead me...please lead me...by Your Holy Spirit, and help me to trust You like the Monroes do. Thank You again. In Jesus's Name. Amen."

Holly had forgotten something and had come back down the hall just as Chris began to pray and had stopped in the doorway at the family room. His prayer had melted her heart and as the tears began to roll down her cheeks, she turned and went back down the hall to bed, completely forgetting what she had gone back for. "Yes, God, thank You *so* much...for everything. You truly are an awesome God," she said quietly as she turned over and closed her eyes in blissful sleep.

Chris made a sandwich, sat down at the table, and for the first time in his life, he bowed his head and asked God to bless the food for which he was truly grateful and meant it with all his heart. Such a simple thing, but it felt so good to him. He felt so clean. This was a new feeling to Christopher Terrence Lapp, Jr. He knew his life was beginning all over again. For the first time in his life he understood the term "born again."

CHAPTER FOURTEEN

Holly awoke the next morning feeling rested and at peace with everything and everyone in her life. Even the aftermath of the storm, still a long way from cleaned up, couldn't take away all the happiness that God had showered her with the day before. The sun was bright and the promise of a new day awaited. "Your mercies never stop. They are new every day," she sang her own paraphrase of one of her favorite verses quietly as she showered and dressed. *Ah, now I remember what I was going back to the kitchen for last night*, she thought to herself. *I was going to set the coffee pot to start at 8:00.* She quietly slipped down the hall, opened the family room and kitchen curtains and peeked out at her flowers, a daily ritual that she had forgotten in all the recent upset until today. It gave her peace to see the beauty that God had blessed her with. She noticed a little something different in a few areas of her beds this morning and wondered what had happened. She opened the deck door and went out to investigate. It only took a moment to realize that with all the wind and blowing debris, some of her flowers had been damaged...and someone had fixed them. She would find out sooner or later who the Good Samaritan was. For now, she let it lie. She picked several that had broken stems but were still pretty and went back inside. As she stepped back through the deck door, she heard someone in the shower. She went back into the kitchen, put the flowers in a vase, and readied breakfast. Just as she was about to wake the men, Stephen appeared in the family room rubbing, stretching, and sniffing the air.

"Ah, coffee. Lemme at it." He poured a cup and sat down at his place at the table. "I slept like a log," he sighed contentedly.

"Oddly enough, I did, too," Holly confessed as she bent to kiss him. Usually after a day of extreme excitement she would lay awake for hours. "You want to go wake Keith and Chris? I think we're ready to eat," Holly said as she placed the flowers in the middle of the table.

In a few minutes, Chris and Keith strolled into the kitchen stretching and rubbing their eyes.

"Did you boys sleep well?" asked Holly as she set the syrup on the table. She had taken out yet another one of the little pitchers from her collection, a yellow one this time, and filled it with syrup she had warmed for the pancakes.

"Yeah," Keith yawned as he leaned to kiss his mother on the cheek. "Like a baby. I must have been more tired than I thought."

"Not me," Chris mumbled. "I didn't know becoming a Christian could have such an effect on a person." Stephen and Keith smiled and Holly laughed out loud.

"Go ahead...laugh it up. Guffaw at my expense," he teased.

"Have trouble *falling* asleep or *staying* asleep?" Holly asked.

"Both!" Chris complained. "I was excited one minute and the next minute I was thinking of all I have to do...you know, people to meet with, loose ends to tie up. Connections to make...and break," he added thoughtfully. He noticed movement outside the kitchen window and perked up as he said, "Rose and Michael are pulling into the driveway."

"Bet they haven't eaten yet. I'll set a place for them," Holly said as she opened the cabinet and took down two more plates. Keith got flatware and napkins and handed them to Holly as he took his seat at the table. Just then the back door opened and Rose and Michael came in.

"Yum! Got enough for two more?" Rose asked cheerfully. Thankfully, Holly had cooked enough for an army.

Holly motioned for them to sit down and said excitedly, "Wait till you hear the news! Chris, tell 'em!" She pointed to Chris as she sat down and chirped, "I don't know how I could be happier."

Rose and Michael looked at each other and laughed aloud. "We do!" they both blurted out. Then Rose yelled, "How about a New Year's grandchild?" Stephen screamed like a girl and he and Holly jumped up at the same time and ran to hug the happy couple.

Keith said, "Uh-UH!" and then, "I'm going to be an uncle!" and jumped up to join the hugs. Chris sat for a moment laughing at the sight and got up to give hugs and congratulations all around. He thought as he sat back down, *I've acquired a loving family, become a Christian, and now there's going to be a baby. Can life get any better?* He loved children but had so little opportunity to spend time with any.

"I can't believe it!" Holly squealed with delight and clapped her hands. Stephen pulled her close to his side and said, "What say, Granny?"

She playfully elbowed him in the ribs and said, "I'm too young for any of those granny-type names. It'll have to be something cute..." she stopped to think then added, "...like 'Hollygram' or something like that."

"Hollygram!" Keith dropped his jaw.

"Just kidding, son," Holly answered, patting his shoulder. They all talked about whether it would be a boy or a girl, the likelihood of twins, family names, and speculated about who the baby would look like. The conversation continued until they were almost finished eating and Rose said, "What's Chris's news?"

"Oh, my goodness!" Holly gasped as she looked at Chris. "In all the hullaballoo about the baby, we forgot! Chris, I'm so sorry."

"Oh, that's okay," he said shyly. "It's not like you hear you're going to have your first grandchild every day!"

"As great as your news is, Chris's is better! Go ahead, Chris. Tell 'em!" Keith urged as he elbowed Chris's arm.

"Okay," Chris began. "Well, you see, it's like this," he said matter-of-factly. Then he uncharacteristically blurted out, "I became a Christian yesterday!"

Rose and Michael were stunned. Their mouths flew open and they looked at each other then jumped from the table and ran to Chris, smothering him in handshakes, hugs, and pats on the back. "I can't believe it!" Rose almost whispered. "This is so wonderful! I can't believe you let us go on and on and didn't interrupt to tell this!"

"Well, your news was kinda special, too," Chris said with a wink and a smile, folding his arms in front of his plate.

Rose and Michael continued to be awed as Chris and Stephen retold the story of Chris's salvation. As the story ended Stephen said, "This is really good practice for you, Chris. When we get saved we're supposed to tell people. You've been saved less than 24 hours and you've already told the story twice! You'll be ready for testimony time at church in no time!"

They were amused at Stephen's teasing, but Holly said, "Now Stephen, don't push. He'll have plenty of opportunities I'm sure to tell his story as he begins to make changes in his life when he goes home." The thought occurred to her that he might have a hard time finding a church he could attend and be comfortable back home in Los Angeles. "Do you know of any churches you can visit where you won't be mauled every time you walk in the door?"

"Nah. I've been thinking about that and I guess I'll have to check on that with some of the Christian actors I know of out there. I guess I'll need to follow along after them for awhile until I get my bearings. Wow...I'm going to miss having you folks with me when I go home." He hesitated as he bit his lip. "Actually, it's a little scary to think of being on my own out there. Sorta like being thrown to the wolves." He stopped and stared into his coffee cup, deep in thought.

"Chris? You okay?" Michael queried with a frown.

"Oh, yeah," Chris answered. "I was just thinking about the time I played a guard who escorted the Christians to the arena and fed them to the lions in 'Lost Fellows.' I have a lot of overcoming to do. Lots of bad roles to make up for."

"Remember that God has forgiven all of that and put it far from His thoughts. We are more than conquerors. Remember that. The devil will try to rake you over the coals because of your past. You just need to remember that his future is still coming...and he knows it...and he wants to take as many of us with him as he can...believers as well as unbelievers! If you need a hand with the fight, you just call me anytime, day or night. You have my cell number and my e-mail address... use them if you need to."

"That goes for all of us, man," Michael added with a nod and a smile, dark eyes shining.

Holly's heart was suddenly warm at how her family had taken to Chris and accepted him as a part of their family. Seeing them treat him as a son and a brother brought tears to her eyes. She blinked them back and rose to clean up the table before anyone could notice. With her head down in fake concentration on her task she said, "That's right, Chris, you know who to call anytime...for any reason." She turned with her hands full and headed toward the sink, glad to have escaped their scrutiny. Everyone else pitched in and the table was clean in no time. The dishwasher had been unloaded earlier, and Holly filled it as Rose took care of the rest of the table. The two ladies joined the men in the family room and the conversation turned to Macey.

"Mom, why don't you call the hospital and check on her?" suggested Rose.

"How'd you know what I was thinking?" she replied as she lifted the receiver and dialed. She was soon connected with Macey's room and her eyes brightened as Macey told her she had a great night and the doctor had just signed her release papers. "Great! I'll be down to get you within half an hour!" She hung up the phone as she told the others about her agreement with Macey to stay with her a few days until she could get her strength back. They had decided on that arrangement the day before when she had received the good news from her doctor that things were progressing more rapidly than expected. "At the rate she's healing, she probably won't need me more than a day or two."

"I know this is going to sound strange, but remember when I was telling how I got saved and felt all this compassion?" Chris asked Holly. She nodded. "Well, is it okay if I go with you to the hospital? I mean, I won't go inside or anything, but I could accompany you and wait in the car. Your windows are dark enough that no one will see me well enough to recognize me, and you can call me on your cell phone and let me know when you're coming out with her. Is that okay?"

"Sure it is!" Holly assured him.

"Thanks. This compassion thing is a new feeling for me, but I think it somehow has something to do with helping Macey. I really wanted to see her earlier. Isn't that weird? I don't even know her. I've never even seen her."

"Oh, Chris," Holly started. "It's not weird at all. It's just how life is when you become a Christian... you know, 'a new creation.' Sometimes you just want to take action. Some people talk about developing a love for everyone they see as soon as they are saved. No, it's not weird at all. I really like that you feel that way. Just more confirmation that Jesus is working in your life." She smiled and patted his arm as she walked down the hall to put her makeup on. In a few minutes she was back. Chris had had a shower and was dressed and waiting for her. They left, promising to call when they got Macey home and settled and everyone could come to visit. Macey had told her on the phone that she wanted to see everyone as soon as she got home.

The short drive from the Monroe home to the hospital was uneventful but because Holly was driving, it gave Chris a better look at the destruction the tornado had left behind. He had not been out in the daytime to see what he had been helping with that night. This time he was a different person and saw everything so differently. He ached for the people whose homes were demolished and for the children who had lost all their toys. He made a mental note to do something about that later. He felt for the emergency workers who were working such long hours. He was glad that Stephen was a volunteer and could choose the times when he would help. He had announced that he was going back out to help as soon as he visited with Macey and planned to stay for an extended period this time.

Holly parked the car and told Chris that she was pretty sure this was the exit she would be wheeling Macey through but that she would call him when they were heading out just to let him know for sure. He waited only a short time, then his cell phone rang. It was Holly saying that Macey would be wheeled through the exit soon. Somehow Chris was excited... and a little apprehensive. *New feelings...weird.*

Just then he saw Holly walking beside a wheelchair as it was being pushed to the car by a nurse. The occupant was small and plain, but somehow she took Chris's breath away. Holly opened the door and helped Macey into the front passenger seat next to Chris, who had taken the driver's seat in case he needed to move the car to a different entrance.

"I told them I could walk out under my own steam, but they wouldn't hear of it...wheel chairs are hospital rules," Macey explained as she looked up at Chris.

"Macey, this is Chris Lapp. Chris, this is my cousin Macey Knight."

"It's nice to meet you," Macey smiled and said with her thick Southern accent.

"It's nice to meet you, too," Chris answered with a smile. Her hair was auburn...not red and not brown...just beautiful. Her eyes were the most beautiful shade of brown he had ever seen. Holly had told her that Chris was in the car, so she wasn't surprised to see the movie star waiting to take her home. Neither of them could say anything else. It was obvious that Macey was as taken by Chris as he was by her. Fortunately, Holly was busy getting Macey's belongings settled and didn't notice. Chris was cautious, though. He'd had that effect on women for years and always had trouble identifying the reaction. Was it him they liked or were they simply star-struck?

Holly got in the middle seat of the SUV after depositing Macey's things in the rear seat. As she settled in, she saw the two of them looking at each other, speechless and decided she would slice the thick air with, "Uh, Chris, you can start the car now."

"Huh? Oh. Oh, yeah. Okay," he said as he realized he was staring. "Where to?"

"Oh, shoot! Silly me!" Holly said. "I forgot you don't know where she lives. Want to swap places with me?" They swapped and Holly drove the mile and a half to Macey's house. Macey had not seen the devastation and was in awe of the fact that she could recognize so little of her town. It brought tears to her eyes. Chris offered to take her for a ride around the area when she felt up to it, which she quickly agreed to, stating that it probably wouldn't be long, maybe the next day, and she would want a full tour. That would also give Chris a chance to learn the town.

The drive was short and Holly drove through the old historic neighborhood and up the long driveway to Macey's home, a large older house that Macey had restored to its former stately beauty, white and clean, with green shutters. Holly and Macey had keys to each other's houses, and Holly produced hers as Chris opened the car door and helped Macey out. "Do you need some help? Here," he said, putting an arm out for her to hold on to. As her feet touched the ground and she reached for his arm, her knees buckled and Chris caught her and slipped a strong arm around her waist. "Ooh, let's be careful," he cautioned as he led her away from the car and shut the door. Holly had gone inside and raised the garage door so Macey could come the short way into the house. She knew Macey...she would want to stop in the kitchen and sit down at the table and look at the mail. Holly had collected what little the mailman was able to deliver on foot through all the blocked streets and debris and left it on the kitchen table.

Holly stood holding the door for them. "She's a little weaker than she thought," Chris announced as he led her into the house. As Holly had thought, Macey stopped at the table and took a seat.

"Not much mail," she said.

"Well, the post office has had this little interruption called a tornado," Holly said sarcastically as she strode down the hall to put Holly's things away.

"Cute!" Macey yelled after her, winking at Chris. Turning to him she said, "I guess my mind is still on hospital time...I didn't think about the mail being interrupted."

Chris answered with, "Yeah, there have been lots of things to think about that are just normally taken for granted. Electricity, grocery shopping, pumping gas, getting mail, newspaper delivery...lots of stuff."

"And my puppy and kitty," Macey said softly as a sad look came over her face. "I wonder where they are."

"I looked for them when I came for the mail, but I never saw them," Holly said as she entered the room. She looked at Macey's face and decided to change the subject. "Want to come into the family room and sit where it's more comfortable?" she asked as she went for the refrigerator. "Chris, will you help Macey to her chair while I get us something to drink?" she asked as she opened the door. "Oh, shoot!" she added. "I forgot...your power was off until last night, so I'm not sure about all the stuff in your fridge. I'll clean it out later. We'll just have ice water for now."

Just then the doorbell rang and Rose and Michael came through the back door with a vase of flowers. "Hey, sicko," Rose said as she set the bouquet on the kitchen table. Chris looked at Macey then at Holly then at Rose with a shocked look. "Oh," Rose laughed. "It's a running joke between Macey and me. Whenever I was sick as I was growing up, Macey would bring me flowers and call me 'sicko.' It's an inside joke." Michael was still laughing at the look on Chris's face.

"Man, you're all sickos," Chris said laughing and shaking his head. "Mind if I take a walk around the yard?"

"Help yourself," Macey answered cordially. Chris nodded his thanks and went out to look around. He wanted to see if she had flowers that needed rescuing like Holly's had. He also had in mind that he would look around for a lost cat and dog. Assuming the picture of a calico and a golden retriever he had seen on a shelf in the family room were the missing animals, he thought he'd take a look around for them just in case they were hiding out somewhere.

"Can we do anything for you, Macey?" asked Rose.

"Yeah, I thought I might need to bring my ladder and put a tarp on your roof, but your place looks untouched. I'm kinda surprised, really," added Michael, rubbing the back of his head.

"I certainly am a blessed woman," Macey replied with a sigh. "The place really looks good. You'd never know an F3 had been through, would you?"

"Well, you would if you saw the rest of the town," Holly said grimly.

"And I'm ready to see it...Chris promised me a tour," Macey told Rose and Michael, then added, "If I sleep well tonight, maybe we can do that tomorrow."

"Would you like me to stay with you tonight?" asked Rose. "I know Mom promised to stay with you, but Michael has some things to do, and I really don't, and I'd kinda like to feel useful."

"As a matter of fact maybe you should do that. I was a little weak when I got out of the car to come in, but if I have a good night, I shouldn't need anyone after that." Macey answered.

Since Holly and Macey had talked a lot at the hospital about her trip to The Netherlands and meeting Chris and the good times they'd had, Macey was pretty well caught up on the latest news, but they chatted awhile about how Chris's visit was going with them.

"You know, Stephen led Chris to the Lord yesterday," Michael said.

"No! Why hasn't someone told me?" Macey squealed. "That's wonderful! Can you imagine what that's going to do for people? His fans? His associates? All kinds of people!"

"Yeah, I know," Holly squealed back. "I can hardly believe it."

Just then the back door opened and a different kind of squeal emerged from the kitchen...then a meow. Their eyes grew wide and Rose said, "You don't think..."

Then Macey yelled, "Candy! Fido!"

As Chris brought Macey's missing pets into the room, he looked at Michael and said, "No, it's not..." to which Michael answered, "Yes, it is...the dog's name is Fido."

"Macey..." Chris said flatly as he turned to her.

"I know it's not original," she whined, "but I just thought it would be fun to have a dog named 'Fido.' You gotta admit, though, that 'Candy' is not your basic common cat name."

"Well, ya got me there," Chris answered, taking a seat on the couch.

"Where did you find them?" Macey asked, stroking her pets as they nestled in her lap, obviously glad to see her. "Did you wonder where I had been?" she asked them.

"They love her so much I half expect them to answer her," Holly said smiling. Chris explained that the elderly couple next door had found them the night of the storm hidden behind their pool house, covered in debris that had blown from the next neighborhood. Like Macey's house, Macey's neighborhood had not been touched by the storm.

"God does work in mysterious ways His wonders to perform," Chris said. This surprised the others, and it showed on their faces. "It was a line I had to say in a movie about ten years ago," he explained. "Who knew I'd say it with true conviction ten years later?" he shrugged. He took the opportunity to practice what Stephen had told him: Tell someone. So he told Macey the story of how he had come to be saved the day before.

"Wow," she said happily. "I'm so glad for you, Chris. You'll never regret it."

"I know," he said quietly. "I know."

They finished their visit and left with Rose promising to be back shortly with her necessities for spending the night. Holly promised to return later and clean out the fridge, which she did and restocked it as well. Rose returned soon, Holly bid them both good night and headed home.

She went into her house to find Stephen, Keith, and Chris talking in the family room. "Hey, honey," Stephen called as Holly dropped her purse on the kitchen table and let out a breath.

"Tired, Mom?" Keith asked sympathetically.

"Yeah, it's been an exhausting couple of days," she replied as she dropped onto the couch beside Chris.

"Hungry? We have some leftovers," Stephen offered. "I'll even warm them up for you."

"No, thanks," Holly answered waving him off with her hand and popping a piece of chewing gum into her mouth. "I think I took a bite out of everything I put into Macey's fridge."

"Then here's hoping you didn't stock her up with raw meat," Chris teased.

"Actually, I did throw in some ground turkey and hot dogs...and I did eat one of the hot dogs right out of the package! Not my day for raw ground turkey, though."

"Blech!" said Keith rolling his tongue over his bottom lip.

"I thought you'd never get here," Stephen said to Holly as he reached behind the sofa and produced a bag from the local Christian book store. "I have a presentation to make," he said as he handed the bag to Chris and set a box of tissues on the coffee table. "With love, from the Monroe family. Really from Papa Monroe," he said with a grin.

Chris took the bag slowly, searching Keith's and Holly's faces for some hint as to what was going on, encountering blank stares and shrugs from each. "Go ahead. Open it," Keith said. "If it's a gift from Dad, it's a good one." Chris reached into the bag and brought out a box wrapped in brown and navy striped paper and topped with a navy bow. He looked at Stephen quizzically. Stephen just sat with a satisfied smile. Chris slowly pulled off the bow and tore off the paper. He took the lid off the box and pulled back the folds of tissue paper revealing a black leather-bound book that said, "Holy Bible" in gold on the front. At the bottom right corner in the same gold lettering, but smaller, it read, "Christopher Terrence Lapp, Jr." He swallowed hard and looked at Keith, then Holly and finally at Stephen.

"Open the cover," Stephen said quietly smiling. A hush fell over the room as Chris opened the cover and read aloud the message Stephen had penned on the inside.

"I know, in the past, life has been hard for you, growing up without parents, being passed around from pillar to post, never having a real home or feeling the love of a family; but your adoption is sure and complete now, not only with Jesus but with us. You have a family that loves you and always will, not only the Monroe family but the family of God. He is your Heavenly Father, and He has given me to be your spiritual father, and I will do my best to make Him proud of me and to do right by you. You will always be welcome with us. I love you." Beneath that, Stephen had signed his name, Stephen Caldwell Monroe.

No one moved. No one said a word. Complete silence. Holly reached for a tissue and handed it to Chris, whose cheeks were streaming with tears, before plucking one for herself and setting the box back on the table. "I don't know what to say," Chris said as he wiped his eyes.

"Say, 'Thank you,'" Keith teased with shiny eyes.

"Thank you, Stephen. It's beautiful...not just the Bible, but the message."

"I mean every word of it, son," replied Stephen as he stood. Chris came to him and they hugged, like father and son. Stephen towered over Chris making him appear to be the child he felt like right now. Chris couldn't remember much about his own parents who loved him so much as they had died when he was so young. Having parents, even spiritual ones, was so new to him, but he liked it because they were so loving and didn't condemn him for the life he had led. Instead, they had led him into a new life, a better one. The best one. "Keep this Book close to you. It'll become a good friend."

"I will," Chris promised as he rubbed his hand across its leather front.

Stephen changed the subject. "There's one aspect of your new life that we haven't touched on yet."

"Yeah?" Chris asked.

"Yeah. Your water baptism," Stephen replied. "Ever been to a baptism?"

"Yeah. My grandfather made us go to a couple when I was little."

"Do you know the significance?"

"No. Not at all."

"It's an outward sign that you have become a Christian. You've already prayed to become a Christian, but this is like sealing the deal publicly. I've been thinking...why don't we call our pastor over to the Bakers' pool one day before you go back to Los Angeles and you can be baptized? It would be private enough so that you wouldn't be gawked at by folks whose motives might be less than sincere, but there would be enough of us there to make it public...and the Bakers would be thrilled. They had that pool put in years ago for the neighborhood when Rose and Keith and some of the other kids were little so they would have somewhere to swim. There have been many baptisms, graduation parties, birthday parties, church youth parties, and other gatherings at that pool, and the Bakers would be honored to add your baptism to the list of happy times they've shared."

"Okay. Sounds great," Chris agreed.

Stephen explained what would happen. They would all gather at the pool, the pastor and Chris would go into the pool, the pastor would say that Chris had become a Christian and was making it public and would immerse him and say something like, "I now baptize you, Chris Lapp, in the Name of the Father and the Son and the Holy Spirit. Chris would come up out of the water and everyone would clap.

They discussed the details and agreed to call their pastor and the Bakers the next day and set it up.

Chris said, "I talked with some of my folks back in L.A...."

"Lower Alabama?" Keith asked with an innocent look.

"Oh, brother," replied Chris shaking his head. Stephen rolled his eyes as he said, "Keith, that joke is moldy."

"I know, but it always gets a rise out of *somebody*."

"Go on, Chris," Holly said as she wadded her chewing gum paper and threw it at Keith, who caught it and threw it at the small decorative wastebasket across the room. It went in and Keith raised his arms in victory and shouted, "He scores!"

"Anyway..." Holly turned her attention back to Chris. Then Chris explained that he had talked with his agent, Lorne, and set up an appointment to talk with him at his office in Los Angeles in a couple of days.

"Oh, no, you're leaving?" Holly sat up and looked sad and shocked at the same time.

"Well, Holly, you had to know I would eventually have to leave!"

"Well, yeah, I know, but so soon," she whined. "We're gonna miss you."

"Believe me, I'm gonna miss you guys, too, but I'll come back and visit."

"You know you're welcome here any time. I HOPE you know that. We're your spiritual parents now, and you should know that you can come here whenever you want to. Just call to be sure we're gonna be here before you buy plane tickets!"

"Okay, here's a little thing I've been thinking about in that department, since you mention plane tickets." He turned to Stephen and asked, "Do you remember telling me on our walk that you had always wanted your pilot's license but really saw no reason to get it since at that time your wife wouldn't fly? Remember telling me that?"

"Yeah?" Stephen answered with a questioning lilt in his voice.

"Remember I told you I have a plane?" Without waiting for an answer he continued, "Well, it's a new plane, and I don't have a pilot yet, and I'd like to pay for you to get your pilot's license. Then I'd like you to be my pilot. What do you say?"

Stephen was stunned and his mouth dropped open to prove it. "Are you serious?" He had been out all day with the police and sheriff's departments helping with the tornado aftermath and was really tired, but suddenly he got a second wind.

"I'm very serious," Chris said with a sincere look. Holly and Keith looked at each other and grinned, each knowing that Stephen must be soaring already. It had been a dream of his to get his pilot's license for decades, and he wasn't sure he was hearing correctly.

"W-w-well, let me pray about this while you're gone and see what God says. I'd love to, but I want to ask Him what He wants me to do."

"Fair enough," Chris said. "I'll give you a few days."

They talked for awhile about things of the Lord, the people Chris would try to be in contact with back in Los Angeles and what he'd have to say to them, when he might be able to come back, and various and sundry other items of interest before retiring for the evening.

"Mom, is your computer on?" Keith asked. "Yeah, honey, go ahead," she answered with a yawn as she followed Chris and Stephen down the hall. Keith headed for Holly's office. "I'm just going to check my e-mail, then I'm going to bed."

"Okay, honey, lock up, would you?"

"Sure, Mom. Good night."

"Good night, baby."

Holly and Stephen went into their bedroom after saying, "Good night," to Chris. "Well, honey, what do you think of Chris's offer?" Holly asked with a grin as she drew her pajamas from the dresser drawer.

"I don't know what to think. I think I'm still in shock. Do you know how long I've wanted this?" he asked rubbing the back of his neck.

"Here. Sit down," Holly said as she sat on the bed. Stephen sat down on the edge of the bed and Holly rubbed his neck as they discussed whether Stephen's dream would come true.

"I haven't prayed yet, but I have a good feeling about this," Stephen said. "Thanks, honey. That really makes my neck feel better," he said with a peck on her cheek as he got up and readied himself for bed.

They lay in bed talking for awhile and each went to sleep with happy thoughts, praying for God's will to be done in all their lives but specifically for His guidance about Chris's generous offer. *Such a nice guy,* Holly thought as she drifted off to sleep. Naturally, it took Stephen a little longer. He was keyed up but finally fell asleep and dreamed of signing on the dotted line and receiving his first flying lesson. Fortunately, there was a flying instructor at their airport, small as it was. If God gave the "go ahead," he'd sign up with him.

CHAPTER FIFTEEN

Chris had been such a help over the past few days, helping clean up the basement, taking Macey for the promised tour of the tornado's path of destruction, and doing lots of other things. It had truly taken hardly any time at all for him to become just like one of the family.

His baptism had been planned for the last day of his visit, and, as expected, the Bakers were ecstatic about having it in their pool. It had been a happy day for Chris and his new family, as well as Macey, the pastor, and the Bakers. Of course, Sue Baker had cooked a feast to celebrate and everyone had enjoyed the day. The experience seemed to strengthen Chris's faith even more.

The next day when it was time to take Chris to the airport, Stephen and Keith stayed behind to continue in the tornado recovery effort in Wells, as did Rose and Michael.

Holly and Chris enjoyed a pleasant trip to Atlanta, and as they exited the expressway and entered the airport parking lot, Chris caught a glimpse of something pink by the roadside and turned around to see what it was. Holly asked if something was wrong. The fact was that on a stroll outside the Monroe home after his baptism the day before, he had walked past the terra cotta pot of pink petunias, and somehow it had triggered a memory he had long forgotten.

"No, no. I just saw a pink flower by the road and it reminded me that I had forgotten to tell you this. As I was walking around your yard yesterday, I finally figured out why your petunias have haunted me so much.

"Yeah?"

"See, when I was about three years old, I had this favorite little book that I used to bug my mother to read to me pretty much on a daily basis. It was mostly pictures and had a big picture of pink petunias in a terra cotta pot. The day my parents were killed, my mother read me the book and we went to a nursery and bought some pink petunias and a terra cotta pot, and she and I planted the flowers and set them in the sun on our back porch. Then we went inside and had a big piece of chocolate cake and a glass of milk. She picked me up and held me tight and told me she loved me very much and kissed me on the cheek. Then we sat in the big rocking chair and she read me the little book again." He looked down, rubbed his hands together, and looked out the window. "It was the last time I ever saw her."

The story touched Holly's heart and her eyes welled up. She blinked the tears away so that she could see how to drive. "Chris, I'm so sorry." She swallowed hard. "But I'm glad you have that memory of your mother. I wish we could somehow put it on tape so you could keep it forever. I'm so sorry you lost her and your father...and so tragically."

"Yeah, I know," he answered quietly, "but you know what? It's sorta symbolic, really. To me, the newly planted flowers represent new life. My real mother left my life, leaving behind that promise of new life, and my spiritual mother entered my life carrying that promise." Holly pulled up to the curb at the airport, choking back the tears as she listened to his interpretation of the symbolism in the story.

"That's really beautiful," she said quietly. They sat still for a moment, then, through misty eyes Holly said, voice cracking, "I can't believe you're leaving." She had held it in as long as she could and she began to weep. His eyes began to fill with tears. "Oh, let's stop this," she said snatching a tissue from the box in the back seat and waving it around. They got out and he pulled his bags from the vehicle. They walked to the baggage check and Holly said, "Unfortunately, this is the end of the line for me." Then she smiled and said, "It's been such fun having you around and getting to know you. My head is still spinning from all the activity of the last few days, and I know yours must be, too, considering all that's happened with you lately. You're a pleasant house guest and easy to be around...and a wonderful new addition to our family. Please come back soon. *Please*."

"Holly," Chris began. "You and your family are the sweetest people I've ever known. I really mean that, and you know it. You've become my family. I appreciate so much your letting me come to your home and make it mine. You know I can't stay away from you and your family for long." With that he put his arms around her and squeezed her tightly. She hugged him back, tears streaming. He stepped back and wiped her tears with his hands. "I'll be back...probably sooner than you think." He picked up his bag and kissed her on the cheek. "Bye, Mom," he said with a wink and walked through the door into the airport. After several days of freedom to be himself, it was necessary to don the disguise again, and Holly watched the sunglasses and new Braves baseball cap, a going-away gift from Rose and Michael, disappear through the doors as they opened and closed around the famous man.

As he disappeared into the busy terminal, Holly thought to herself how cryptic the last part of the conversation was. "...probably sooner than you think." She wondered why he had said that. He had said nothing earlier to indicate that he would be coming back for a visit soon, only that he would come back for a visit. The thought lingered throughout the three-hour drive back home, even when she stopped at her favorite roadside stand for freshly picked strawberries. The farmer never seemed to charge enough, and she always gave him a larger bill and told him to keep the change. The berries were always so plump and sweet and made for delicious strawberry cobblers. She wished Chris could be here to help them eat the one she would prepare tonight. She missed him already. He had gotten along so well with the whole family, even Macey, whom he had only known for the last few days.

On the plane, Chris, too was thinking of Macey. He couldn't help it. He was drawn to her. He thought about how he had wanted to meet her, the compassion he had felt before he had even known her, the desire he had to help her. What *was* that? As he sat, he prayed silently, *Lord, thank You for my new life...for making me a new creation...for my new family.* He had said this to God every day since his salvation. *God, I can't get Macey off my mind. What's going on?* Then, as he lay his head against the window, a scripture flashed before his closed eyes. He opened them with a start. What was that? Jeremiah 29:11? *Was that You, Lord?* He had brought his new Bible on board the plane and had intended to use the down time to acquaint himself with it. That in itself was going to be a new experience, but he had not thought the process would start quite like this. He retrieved the precious tome from his carry-on and opened the front cover, noticing Stephen's handwriting, and knew he had to quickly turn the page or he would go all emotional again. He hoped that would soon go away. He didn't want to cry every time he opened his Bible!

Jeremiah, Jeremiah, Jeremiah...where is that? Is that the Old Testament or the New Testament, I wonder? "Old Testament," he seemed to hear. He knew it wasn't a voice but almost like he had actually heard something. He looked around. Everyone around him was either sleeping or reading. *Hmmm...strange.* He looked around again. *Okay, I'll look in the Old Testament.* His quick eyes scanned down the first column of Old Testament books in the Table of Contents then to the next column.

Psalms, Proverbs, Ecclesiastes, Song of Songs, Isaiah... ah, Jeremiah. He turned to page 1053 to find Jeremiah then turned several pages to find Jeremiah 29:11 and read silently, "'For I know the thoughts that I think toward you,' says the Lord, 'thoughts of peace and not of evil, to give you a future and a hope.'" He considered what he had read for a minute or two. Stephen and Holly had both, at separate times, told him that God has a plan for his life, and here it was from God Himself. He looked back at the verse. "...to give you a future and a hope." He wondered if this future would include Macey. He promised himself that he would pray about this every day. He also promised himself that he would begin to memorize scripture, and he couldn't think of a better time to start than now. With that, he reread the scripture and immediately committed it to memory.

"God has given you talents that he wants you to use for Him," Holly had once told him.

Ah...I see now, Lord. You've given me the ability to memorize things sometimes with only a couple of readings, and this is one of the things you want me to use it for. I'll do it gladly, he promised as he closed the precious Book. He realized that Bible reading was going to be a wonderful new way of life for him. In the days to come, he would look forward to it more and more and would prove to be a very quick study, not only committing scripture to memory but also becoming aware of its meaning for his life. Jesus quickly became his friend, Someone he loved very much. How grateful he was for the flight to Amsterdam and the new friends and new life...and the family...it had brought him.

Back in Los Angeles he reacquainted himself with his sprawling mansion. It had been several weeks since he had been here, and he just wanted to relax for awhile. He had really enjoyed being a houseguest of the Monroe family back in Wells, Georgia, but Dorothy was right: There certainly is no place like home. He took a couple of days to think and pray and make plans and lists of people to contact about various points of business. His new life beckoned him to make some changes...changes he knew were going to affect his life forever but in a way that he also knew would help transform him into the man that Jesus desired him to be.

Having decided against contacting his management people separately, he canceled his appointment with Lorne and arranged a lunch meeting at his own home with his business manager and personal manager, as well as Lorne. Others were invited who had prior engagements, but he was sure he would meet with them eventually.

He knew the points he needed to address at this luncheon, the most important of them being that he had become a born-again Christian and that some changes would have to be made in all aspects of his life. He knew this was going to hit them like a lightning bolt, and he wasn't sure exactly how they would receive it; but he knew it was right. He had never been "righter" about anything in his life. He knew that. If they couldn't accept and work with him in this new light, they would have to part ways. If that were the case, he hoped it would be amicable. He was going to use this, though, as an opportunity to tell them how to become Christians. It excited him to think of what might happen, but he knew that it might not go exactly the way he...or the Lord...would like it to go. *"Lord, please, You be in control,"* he had prayed earlier.

The day arrived for the meeting and his kitchen staff had come through, as usual, with a delectable spread in the luxurious dining room. The noonday sun filtered through the starched ivory sheers that hung between the imported draperies of crimson damask on all the windows. The walls were covered in French wallpaper of navy and crimson toile. The sideboard, massive china display cabinet, banquet table, and chairs were of fine mahogany, the seats covered in solid crimson damask to match the drapes. Chris knew his maternal grandparents had been drapery and cornice makers and insisted that every window in the house carry a cornice above it and fine draperies on each side, even the eight bathrooms. In each corner of the room stood a different tall green plant, meticulously cared for by Sage, the old gentleman who lived there and watched over the grounds when Chris was away. Chris had found him on the streets in Phoenix while shooting a movie a couple of years earlier. He had befriended him and taken him in because Sage's situation reminded Chris of his own brief stint on the streets at the onset of life on his own. Sage was humble and grateful for Chris's act of kindness and had always been faithful to care for Chris's house and grounds as if they were his own when Chris was away.

The guests had arrived in a relatively timely fashion and Chris ushered them into the dining room, inviting them to take their seats at the table. An arrangement of bright yellow King Alfred daffodils had been placed in the center of the table, and its perfume filled the air. A variety of salad dressings rested in a silver tray beside it. In each golden charger, a crisply starched crimson napkin had been placed, neatly folded into thirds, displaying the initials CTL centered and monogrammed in navy script. As the guests placed their napkins in their laps, the food was served.

A green salad was placed at each plate. A plain white china plate with steamed vegetables, a thick slab of prime rib, and a baked potato was set inside each charger. A basket of freshly baked yeast rolls and butter was placed on the other side of the flowers, and a serving cart was wheeled in with pitchers of iced tea and water on the top shelf. A tray of Marlene's decadent homemade desserts was placed on the sideboard alongside a silver coffee set complete with pot full of steaming coffee and all the required accompaniments. Chris knew this wasn't normal lunch fare, more like dinner, but hoped his guests would be more inclined to swallow his good news if they had first swallowed his good food.

"Thank you, Marlene," Chris smiled as the tall heavy-set gray-haired lady left the room. She returned his smile and shut the heavy double doors behind her. There was something different about Chris since she had last seen him, but she just couldn't put her finger on it.

Chris had asked for the drinks and desserts to be left at the beginning of the meal so that there would be no reason for their luncheon to be disturbed. He knew this was going to be a difficult meeting, and he wanted their full attention without interruption or distraction.

"Enjoy," he invited as he picked up the small tray of dressings and passed it to his left. Lunch progressed with a steady stream of pleasantries and the usual Hollywood gossip, which was now boring to Chris. The guests expressed their satisfaction with the meal, a couple of them rising to refill their glasses. They were just beginning to partake of the lemon pie and tiramisu when Lorne, his agent, decided it was time to cut to the chase.

"Chris, it was nice of you to have this little luncheon, but why are we really here?"

Chris had finished his meal, his appetite slightly on the wane at the moment, and folded his napkin, placing it beside his plate. He quickly, silently asked God to help him do this in a way that would be pleasing to Him. He had already prayed and prayed the night before and this morning, asking God to let him see at least one at the luncheon come to Him, but he felt the need to ask God's help one more time.

"Something has happened to me that is going to affect all of us, something wonderful, something that has changed my life forever...and I hope yours, too."

Okay, he had gotten their attention. All eyes were fixed on his, some suspicious, some expectant, some blank.

"My life has been empty for longer than I realized until my recent trip to The Netherlands," he began. "I met someone who is the closest thing to a mother than anyone in my life since my real mother died when I was three. And she introduced me to Someone that has changed my life."

As he took a moment to breathe, Lorne's eyebrows raised as he said, "You met a girl."

Chris laughed and said, "It's bigger than that."

"Whoa, this IS serious," his business manager, Sandra, said, eyebrows arched to the max.

"Well," Chris nodded. "You got that right." He paused and looked around the table into the eyes of each person. "I became a Christian. I met Jesus Christ on this trip."

No one moved for a moment. "You can exhale now," Chris smiled. Nervous laughter peppered the setting.

"What are you saying, Chris?" asked Lorne. His voice betrayed the apprehension he was feeling.

"I'm saying that I became a Christian, and I've never been happier in my life. My life has taken on meaning, really for the first time in my three-plus decades.

"Does that mean you're going to quit acting and become a priest?" He should have anticipated the query from his personal manager, Dale, who had been raised in a staunch Catholic family.

"No, no," Chris quickly answered. "That's not the way it works." Thankful that he had been praying and reading his Bible so much lately he explained that the Bible says that you don't have to drop everything you're doing and run off to "do the Lord's work," but that you should continue your day-to-day life until...and if...God calls you to something else. "Now I WILL have to make a lot of changes in my lifestyle and in the choices of roles I accept. I realize now that I have done some pretty raunchy stuff over the years that I wish I could take back, but all I can do is apologize, ask forgiveness, and move on to better things. So at this time I ask your forgiveness for all the times I've led you...all of you...into the gutter, either by my speech or by my actions or by luring you into doing things that you might not have done otherwise. I know that many times you have participated in some pretty unsavory actions that you might not have been a part of except that you were with me. For that I am truly sorry. I won't lead you down those roads again...ever."

Lorne squinted his eyes and pursed his lips as he asked,"You're not going to go all boring on us, are you, guy?"

"Boring?!" Chris blurted and laughed. "One thing the Christian life is not and that is boring! In the last couple of weeks I have flown to The Netherlands, met a woman who introduced me to the Person I've needed all my life, found out that flowers and cheese can make some people enormously happy, lived through a tornado, helped rescue people in the darkness of it all, made some of the most wonderful friends in the world, found the family I never had, discovered some new feelings that I've never known, and, best of all, I've found my Savior. All because of a Christian family. Uh...NO...I'm not going to be bored OR boring!'"

"Flowers and cheese, Chris?" Sandra asked quietly with a sarcastic look on her face.

"Oh, Sandy, you know...the simpler things in life. With Holly it was flowers and cheese in The Netherlands, with other people it's animals, with others it's volunteering, with others it's spending time with family, you know...the simpler things in life. For years I've had all this, this..." He waved his arms over his head and around his sides as he searched for words. "*Stuff*...this house, the cars, the money, the women, the booze, the drugs. Everything that Hollywood has had to offer, I've been a part of. And none of it has made me happy. None of it has filled this empty place in my life, in my heart. None of it has made me stop and think about what my life has been about, or what it should be about." He stopped and realized that this was the perfect place to make his plea for their salvation through Jesus Christ. Quietly he added, "And none of it has made me realize that I was on the fast track to Hell. The life I was leading was pushing the truth farther and farther away from me...and the truth is that I was a sinner. You can laugh if you want to, but I'm telling you, sin is real, Hell is real, but so is the fact that you and I can be forgiven of all our sins. Our slates can be wiped clean. Mine has been, and I'm never going back to who I was before. I'm becoming something...someone...more than that. And that can only be done by realizing that I'm a sinner, confessing that to Jesus Christ, and asking Him to come and save me and help me live my life for Him, in a way that's pleasing to Him. I've done that, folks, and it's the best thing I ever did...better than acting, better than making money, better than racking up all these 'important contacts,'"...he glanced at his agent and smiled. "Better...just...*better*. I like the new me. I hope you will, too, but more than that, I love Jesus Christ, and I'd like you to know Him and love Him, too."

Everyone was quiet for a long time. Chris was patient. He had learned patience recently and liked its effect on him.

Sandra broke the silence. "But I'm Jewish, Chris."

"Yeah, and I'm Catholic," Dale chimed in.

"And I just don't care," Lorne said with an uncomfortable shrug.

"That would make you an agnostic," Dale said with an air of importance.

"It doesn't matter what you are or aren't," Chris said as he rose and walked to the window. He looked out, collecting his thoughts. Turning back to his guests he said, "I've never been surer of anything in my life." He paused. "You guys have known me for how many years now? Do you think this is a whim? No way! This is as real as life gets. I've never had this kind of peace with...with...with anything!" He almost yelled with delight as he threw his hands up in the air. He regained his composure and continued, "Nothing in my life has ever made me feel so alive. And it feels so permanent. That's because it is. I'm never walking away from this." He almost whispered as he leaned on the table with both hands, looked into their eyes, and pled, "Please, please think about what I've said."

His guests were quiet for a couple of minutes, then Dale spoke up. "Look," he said as he rose from his seat and placed his napkin beside his plate. "I have a 2:30 appointment across town, and I can't be late. I gotta run. Thanks for lunch...and for sharing your...story," he added as he reached across the table and shook Chris's hand. Chris nodded and watched him leave the room, his quick steps crossing the flagstone hallway and fading in the distance. He turned back to his remaining guests.

"I gotta go, too, Chris," Sandra almost whispered, a slight smile crossing her lips as she, too, rose from her seat and shook hands with her client. She didn't look back as she exited the open doors.

Lorne was left alone at the table as Chris walked back to his chair and slowly sat down. "Well, that went well, don't you think?" he laughed as he looked into Lorne's eyes, expecting him to laugh. He always laughed at Chris's jokes, but Chris never really knew if it was because he really thought they were funny or if Lorne was just patronizing his client. However, Lorne wasn't laughing now. He was slowly twisting the end of his napkin and looking out the window across from him, squinting at the afternoon sun streaming in, filling the room with its brilliance and warmth. Chris strode over to the window and closed the sheers which were just thick enough to block some of the bright light. He turned back to Lorne, who was still twisting his napkin and staring.

"You okay, buddy?" Chris asked, concerned.

"No. No, not at all," was Lorne's soft, slow answer. Chris had noticed that Lorne looked tired, and his eyes were swollen and dark. "I haven't slept much for several nights now," he confessed. "I think what you've said today makes more sense than I would have ever thought it would. I need you to tell me exactly what happened to you 'cause I need something, man. I'm tired of living this life." Lorne's life was full of all the trappings of the entertainment world, and it was bearing down on him. He had known for a long time that, if he didn't do something about it, he would end up in trouble...or dead.

Silently Chris thanked God for this opportunity and asked Him to speak through him the words that Lorne needed to hear in order to realize that Jesus Christ was what he needed. They sat for two hours as Chris told all about what his life had been like and how Holly and her family had introduced him to Jesus Christ and His love and saving grace and power. He gave him scriptures that explained just what it means to be a sinner in need of a Savior and how Jesus is the only Way to salvation. Lorne knew immediately that this was what he needed, what he wanted. Chris led him in the prayer of salvation. It was like an enormous weight had lifted off of Lorne's shoulders as tears streamed down his face. Chris was elated as he and his friend embraced and wept in silence.

"What do I do now, Chris?" Lorne asked as he produced a white handkerchief from his back pocket and wiped his eyes.

Chris knew immediately and answered him with, "Well, first you need to tell someone."

Lorne looked down and smiled softly as he said, "I know exactly who I'll tell first."

"Yeah?"

"Yeah. My parents," Lorne answered, tears welling up again, as he thought of his dear Christian mother and father back in Omaha who had prayed for his salvation for years.

"Boy, are they in for a surprise!" Chris said loudly, breaking the mood.

Lorne laughed and Chris knew he wasn't just playing along with a client but was indeed joyful at the thought of hearing his parents' exclamations of happiness.

"You and I are brothers now and we're going to find a church where we can get you baptized and where we can learn the Bible together. Hey, maybe we can find you a wife finally!" Chris teased. Lorne punched him on the shoulder as he reached to shake his hand.

"Thanks, man. You're a real friend." Chris saw him to the door and watched him drive away in his red sports car. As he closed the door he thanked God for what had just happened.

It was only after Lorne had accepted Jesus Christ as his Savior and left a new man that Chris realized that there was no way he could have remembered all those scriptures and at the right moments except that the Holy Spirit had brought them back to him in answer to his silent prayer for help in witnessing to Lorne. He also remembered reading that very promise in John 14:26 only yesterday. "But the Helper, the Holy Spirit, whom the Father will send in My name, He will teach you all things and bring to your remembrance all things that I said to you." Chris had won someone to Christ and he felt like he would burst if he didn't tell someone. He knew exactly who he would call, and he took his cell phone from his pocket and pressed the Monroes' number.

CHAPTER SIXTEEN

"Hi, Chris...Uh-UH!...You're kidding!" Keith yelled. Stephen looked up from his newspaper at Keith with a quizzical stare. Holly turned toward Keith and stopped stirring the custard for the banana pudding she was preparing for their dessert.

"Chris?!" she asked, shocked that they were hearing from him so soon. "Wonder what's up?" she whispered to Stephen. Stephen shrugged.

Keith listened for a few minutes then said, "Okay, buddy...I will...you, too. See ya later. 'Bye."

"What? What?" Holly asked impatiently, spoon in midair dripping the creamy pale yellow concoction onto the stove top.

"Seems our man Chris has been witnessing already. He led his agent to the Lord today."

"You're kidding!" Stephen said with a wide grin as he looked at his wife, who stood frozen, her mouth hanging open. Keith walked over to his mother and, with his index finger under her chin, closed her mouth. "You're gonna let in flies, Mom," he said with a chuckle.

"The boy is incredible," she said as she resumed stirring. "What a blessing he's going to be to the Kingdom. I know God is going to use him mightily."

"Sounds as if He's already begun," Keith said as he dropped down onto the sofa.

Just then Rose peeked through the glass in the back door and waved at her mother, who motioned for them to enter. Rose stepped through the door, and Michael followed.

"Hey. What have you folks been up to since we saw you last?" Stephen asked laying the paper aside. *The Wells Courier Times* could wait. He was always willing to drop what he was doing to spend time with his family. It had taken some time to adjust to not having Rose in the house after her marriage, so time spent with her and Michael was precious, and they knew they should spend as much time with Keith as they could now, since he had recently acquired a girlfriend. Sarah was a lovely girl, and they were growing fonder of her every day.

"We've been helping some neighbors get their houses back in order. It's been strange not having a job to go to, but helping people who need a hand has been wonderful. We go to bed every night feeling like we've done something special. Not that we don't feel that way every day, but...oh, I don't know...this is just different," Rose said throwing one hand into the air as she took a seat in the family room. She and Michael were teachers in the Wells County schools, and since the tornado, they didn't have to report to work. The schools didn't suffer much damage, but many homes were affected and many families had been displaced and were living with relatives outside the county. This posed a problem as graduation was supposed to have been two days after the storm had hit, so the details of that situation were still being negotiated.

"Stay for supper?" Holly asked, to which Rose and Michael gladly agreed. They were tired and grateful to have a nice hot meal they didn't have to prepare. When the meal was ready, everyone took their seats at the table and held hands as Stephen asked the Lord's blessing on the family and the food. Of course, the discussion began with Chris's newsy phone call and ran the gamut from the activities of the day to plans for the future, including the baby that was due in a few months, with Rose reporting that she was feeling great and still experiencing no morning sickness. Michael told of their visit with Macey earlier in the day and how quickly she was healing.

As soon as the words were out of his mouth, a tap came at the back door. Keith went to the door and looked through the glass. "It's Macey!" he said, astonished as he opened the door for her. She gingerly climbed the two steps and struck a graceful pose as if taking center stage on Broadway.

"Amazing," Michael said as he shook his head and took a bite of broccoli. He chewed and swallowed then grinned as he pointed his fork at her and said, "I thought I told you to give it another day or two before you were out driving."

"You're not the boss of me!" she said as she put her hands on her hips and shook her hair back, junior-high style. They all laughed and Stephen brought a chair from the dining room, placing it at the breakfast room table so she could join them. "Here ya go. Have a seat. Want something to eat?" he asked.

"No, no. I still have food left from the gigantic meal you folks brought over yesterday, so I had a bite of that before I left. I won't stay long. Curfew and all that."

"Yeah, I'd hate to have to lock you up," Stephen folded his arms, leaned back in his chair, and pretended to be full of himself. Looters and other unsavory types had forced local law enforcement agencies to impose a curfew the day after the tornado. No one knew when it would be lifted.

"Yeah, I'm really scared," Macey smiled sarcastically, rolling her eyes at Stephen. "Anyone heard from Chris since his visit?"

"Funny you should ask," answered Keith. "He just called, and guess what...he led his agent to the Lord today!" Keith was obviously still excited at the news himself.

"Really? No way!" Macey was shocked as she looked around at the smiling, chewing faces. "Well, he certainly wasted no time racking up crowns in Heaven, huh?"

"Yeah. I can't wait to hear him tell it, but that could be awhile, I guess. I still miss him," said Holly ruefully, her voice trailing off.

"Me, too," Macey said quietly.

"I think you miss him for a different reason than the rest of us," Rose said slyly, cutting her eyes toward Michael, who only grinned as he drew his napkin across his mouth.

"What?" Macey's face flushed as she looked around the table. All eyes were on her.

"Have I missed something?" Stephen looked innocently at his wife, who simply shrugged.

"I didn't suspect a thing either until we were visiting with Macey this afternoon and she seemed to be unable to talk about anything else except Chris or some aspect of his visit with us," Rose tattled through a smug grin.

"Uh...I...uh," Macey managed to choke out.

"Busted!" Keith said, pointing a finger at her and laughing. "Yeah, give it up, Macey," Michael said, leaning back in his chair as he laughed. "The cat's out of the bag."

Macey drew a deep breath and sighed with relief. "Well, I might as well, but you'd better not tell Chris!" She pointed a finger around the table. She drew another deep breath and began her simple explanation. "There's really nothing to tell. I'm just attracted to him. I would have never fallen for him before, but the man he is since his salvation is quite attractive." She hesitated and grinned, knowing she was blushing again. "Of course, I never knew him before, but all the stuff I heard about him on TV just doesn't seem to be who he is now. Obviously, his becoming a Christian has had a real impact on his life, as well it should. To tell you the truth, I really would like to get to know him better. You know, spend some time talking with him to see if what I'm feeling is for real...from the Lord. Ya know?"

They all nodded, and Rose said, "I really think the two of you would make a nice couple. The thought had actually crossed my mind several days ago."

"But please...don't anybody call him up and tell him, okay? Promise? If this is from the Lord, He'll tell Chris, too." Her request met with more nods.

They helped Holly clean up the table and retired to the family room where they talked for awhile. Then Rose and Michael announced that they'd better get home and get some sleep so they'd be fresh to help if they were needed the next day.

"Yeah, I suppose I'd better hit the road, too. Wouldn't want to end up in the pokey," she faked a scowl at Stephen as she headed for the door.

Stephen hugged her and said, "You know I wouldn't put the cuffs on too awfully tight."

She punched him in the side with her elbow. "Yeah, right!"

"See ya later, everybody," Holly called after them as they walked to their cars and she closed the door and locked it for the night.

"I think I'll go to the office in the morning for awhile and see what's gathering on my desk," Stephen announced as he and Holly and Keith sat back down in the family room. He had been helping so much with the tornado cleanup that he had neglected the paper work at his office. He hadn't been terribly busy before the storm hit and therefore didn't expect much accumulation, but he wanted to check in just to be sure. He was still grateful that the tornado had done no damage at his office. After awhile, Holly got sleepy and went to bed. Stephen and Keith followed after watching an episode of their favorite detective show.

The next morning the sun-drenched deck was the perfect place for breakfast and they all spent that time reciting their plans for the day. Holly cleaned up the dishes, Stephen headed for the office, and Keith went to his friend Colby's house. Colby had organized a football game with some kids whose houses had been lost to the storm, a sort of morale booster.

"Gonna be any cheerleaders on the sidelines?" Holly gave Keith a sly grin as Keith was leaving.

"There just might be," he answered, returning her grin as he went out the door.

In an hour or so, Stephen called Holly and told her he needed to make a trip to Atlanta and would probably be home around six or so but would call and let her know for sure.

"Hmmm," she pondered aloud as she hung up the phone. "No lunch to fix for Stephen. Keith will no doubt eat with Sarah and his friends. What will I do with my time? This is a rarity indeed." She decided, since there had been some stressful days of late, that she would treat herself to a book. There were several on her night stand that she had not had time for, so this would be the perfect time to lose herself in one of them. She straightened up the house, put in a load of laundry, and settled down with her novel. It was a beautiful story about God's faithfulness to His own, involving a young family, betrayal, patience, and reconciliation.

The day passed uneventfully and around 4:00 p.m. Stephen called and said he'd be in around 6:00. "I'm picking up some barbecue. Why don't you call Rose and Michael and see if they want to join us? Can't have barbecue pork without Rose. You know how she loves the stuff. Might as well invite ol' Macey, too," he added with a chuckle. "You want to whip us up some baked beans and cole slaw to go with it?"

"Sure thing, honey. I'll get on it right now."

Holly hung up the phone then called the others, all of whom jumped at the chance for barbecue. Rose quickly added, "And will you make one of your peach cobblers? That always goes really well with barbecue." Holly could never turn down the request of one of her family members when it came to desserts. She had such a love for making them and was always looking for an excuse to throw one together.

Pretty soon Holly's kitchen was filled with wonderful smells, the dining room table was set to accommodate the larger-than-normal number of guests, and, feeling strangely festive, a bouquet of flowers from her flower beds was placed in the center. "Oh, dear," she said as she stood back and looked at the table. "There's a hole in the middle of that arrangement. Well, I'll go pick a couple more and fill it in after I take the cobbler out of the oven."

Just then Rose and Michael came in with Macey, whom they had picked up along the way. "He just doesn't want me to drive," Macey said as she poked a finger in Michael's back.

"Somebody's gotta take care of you," he retorted as he went to the oven and peeked in. "Ooooh, Rose. Peach cobbler."

"Mmm," Rose smiled as she sniffed its sweet perfume. "Thanks, Mom."

"Anything for the lady in waiting," her mother replied contentedly.

"And the gentleman in waiting?" Michael asked as he leaned his chin on Holly's shoulder, doe eyes looking up expectantly.

"Your favorite ice cream to plop on top," Holly answered as she opened the freezer door revealing Michael's favorite.

"Vanilla. Michael you are so...so...vanilla," Keith teased as he emerged from the bathroom, freshly showered.

"I'll take that as a compliment," Michael said smugly as he sat down in the family room. "So how are you getting along with Sarah. Wedding bells on the horizon?"

"Hey, I move fast, but not THAT fast!" Keith retorted.

Just then the back door opened slightly and Stephen stuck only his face in and announced, "Look what the cat dragged in!" With that he threw open the door, and in walked Chris!

"Chris!" Holly shrieked as she ran and hugged him.

Stephen was walking in the door behind him, his smile seeming to cover his whole face. He told the others, "I love it when I pull one over on her!"

Chris hugged Holly then produced his right hand from behind his back holding two tulips, one red and one yellow. "I asked Stephen to stop at a florist's shop along the way."

"Oh, Chris!" Holly burst into laughter then into tears.

"And a deli!" he laughed as his left hand emerged holding a heavy bag. Holly opened it quickly and held it up. It was a large round cheese encased in a red paraffin wax coating.

"Cheese!" she yelled.

"Gouda!" Chris corrected loudly.

An enormous roar filled the air as all jumped to their feet and rushed the door.

"Let us in, people," Stephen begged as he tried to get one of Chris's bags in and shut the door. Chris had dropped the bag he was carrying and was reveling in the love being poured out on him at that moment.

After the dust settled, they led Chris into the family room where they all sat in amazement as they listened to how Stephen had pulled this off without a clue to anyone else. "Well, he made it pretty easy on me. As I was walking into my office this morning, my cell phone rang and it was Chris saying that he wanted to come for a visit. I asked him when he wanted to come and he said he had a ticket for the next flight from Los Angeles to Atlanta. As it turns out, my desk wasn't piled up at all, so I took off for the airport."

"You're a sneak!" Holly laughed as she hugged her husband. "I'll put these in the vase on the table. It'll fill that hole I was going to fix."

"What do I smell?" Chris asked, eyes wide in expectation and nose turned upward, sniffing the air.

"Mom's peach cobbler," Rose announced licking her lips.

"And baked beans," added Holly as she eased them from the oven.

"Oh, wow. I've missed this," Chris said as he surveyed the spread Holly was arranging on the island in the kitchen.

The meal was so festive one would have thought it was Christmas. Everyone enjoyed the conversation as well as the food. From time to time Macey would look at Chris and catch him looking at her. Of course, this did not escape Rose's and Michael's watchful eyes.

After awhile Holly said, "Enough of this small talk! I'm itching to hear Chris's story of how he won his agent to the Lord! I can't wait another minute!"

Chris laughed, wiped his mouth and folded his napkin, and told of the luncheon that would forever change Lorne's life, as well as his own. He would never forget the day he led his first convert to the Lord. "The others may not have accepted Jesus as their Savior that day, but I'm going to pray for them until they do. I believe they'll come around eventually."

Naturally, the remainder of the evening was full of laughter, jokes, loving punches, and, yes, a few tears. Chris felt as if he had come home. He asked Stephen if he had applied for flying lessons yet, and Stephen proudly said, "I start next week."

Eventually, Rose and Michael had to leave and hugged everyone as they headed out the door.

"Chris, man, it's so good to have you back," Michael said as he hugged him and gave him a brotherly slap on the back.

"Yeah, really good," added Rose hugging him and glancing at Macey as she and Michael went out the door. Macey grinned and blushed, turning her face away.

The rest of them gathered again in the family room to enjoy each other's company, then Keith decided to head for his computer and Holly and Stephen announced that they were going to bed. It had been a tiring but exciting day for them all.

Macey and Chris were left sitting on opposite sides of the family room, Macey on the sofa and Chris in a chair. Macey smiled shyly, feeling a little self-conscious and so afraid she was going to blush again when Chris said, "Mind if I sit with you? I'd like to talk."

Printed in the United States
202333BV00002B/139-1623/P